May's Moon

May's Moon

S. Y. Palmer

OUR STREET BOOKS

Winchester, UK
Washington, USA

First published by Our Street Books, 2015
Our Street Books is an imprint of John Hunt Publishing Ltd., Laurel House, Station Approach,
Alresford, Hants, SO24 9JH, UK
office1@jhpbooks.net
www.johnhuntpublishing.com
www.ourstreet-books.com

For distributor details and how to order please visit the 'Ordering' section on our website.

ISBN: 978 1 78279 780 7
Library of Congress Control Number: 2015934118

A CIP catalogue record for this book is available from the British Library.

This book makes reference to various trademarks, marks and registered marks owned by the
Disney Company and Disney Enterprises, Inc.

Design: Stuart Davies

Printed in the USA by Edwards Brothers Malloy

We operate a distinctive and ethical publishing philosophy in all
areas of our business, from our global network of authors to
production and worldwide distribution.

Dedication
For Josh and Joseph

'You're **BRAVER** than you believe,
and **STRONGER** than you seem,
and **SMARTER** than you think.'
– A.A. Milne, Winnie the Pooh

Acknowledgements

I would like to thank the following people who have helped me get this far with my writing:

To Al, Michelle, Kate, Carla, Ruth, Agnes, Tracey, Nicki and Alan – for your help, humour, inspiration and belief.

To John Hunt Publishing Ltd – for guiding me through the publishing process.

To Josh, Joseph and my parents – for their unconditional love.

And finally to Simon – for giving me the luxury of time to write and space to follow my dreams.

Chapter One

Click. Michael May fastened the last strap on his spacesuit and lifted on his helmet.

'Primary life support system secure?' shouted the bald-headed man in front of him.

'Check!'

'Helmet secure?'

'Check!'

'Suit sealer secure?'

'Check!'

Michael looked around the hangar. Forget Tom Hill's dream of driving a Bugatti Veyron. Forget Darren Fletcher fantasizing about playing left wing for Chelsea. This had to beat the whole lot: for the first time in his life, Michael wished that everyone at home could see him.

'Give me a thumbs up y'all when you're ready,' said the bald-headed man in uniform. 'Then I'll start up the pumps. Any problems just put your hand up and we'll stop.'

As the words still echoed, Michael's legs wobbled underneath him. What if he wasn't any good? What if he messed it up? This wasn't just a dream any more. He really was in America and he really was just about to find out what it felt like to float in space.

Ten gloved thumbs rose into the air and ten helmets momentarily glanced up to a balcony surrounded by a smoked glass screen. Standing behind it were a huddle of adults wearing half-smiles, scanning every movement below them.

Michael filled his lungs slowly, staring at the water stretching out in front of him. His heart thumped like a jackhammer. Surely everyone else could hear it! Suddenly black fans, sounding like giant microwaves, started to whirr in each corner of the hangar.

Bob Sturton, who was in charge, gave his next command. 'I want y'all to move to the edge of the pool now and then I'm gonna turn on the oxygen to your umbilicals.'

With help, Michael and the other children shuffled to the poolside like giant white penguins. A few seconds later, a rush of cool air flooded into his helmet. Michael almost gulped it.

'This is the most important piece of equipment for you guys,' said Bob, picking up a curly tube that led from the back of Michael's spacesuit to a silver box on the wall. 'This is your "primary life support system" or "umbilical" as we call it. This is where your communication and oxygen come from and it must not, under any circumstances, get twisted. When you get down there, you'll see your support divers. These guys are going to be watching you the whole time and are there to help if you get into trouble. Any problems, remember to put your hand up and they'll come straight to you.'

Michael started running through the briefing they'd all had the day before, trying to remember as much as he could. The building they were in now contained something called a 'Neutral Buoyancy Pool' (NBP). Bob had explained to Michael and the nine others in his group, that this was one of the world's largest indoor pools! Longer and wider than an Olympic-sized swimming pool it was also five times deeper and could hold an entire space shuttle cargo bay in it!

Bob looked at his watch and then lifted his arm to signal the start. One at a time the children inched forwards, then stepped from the poolside onto a square platform suspended from a yellow crane by four metal wires. A loud beeping, which reminded Michael of a lorry reversing, rang around the hangar as barriers jolted down on each side of the platform. With another signal from Bob, it started to lower towards the water.

Michael's chest suddenly tightened and his gloves grew damp inside. He couldn't let it affect him now. He just couldn't! He would soon be below the surface and anyway, he was in a spacesuit this time. The water couldn't get to him. Deep breaths – take long, deep breaths, he thought. The jackhammer began to slow and by the time Michael was completely submerged, his breathing was calm again.

He hadn't prepared himself for what it would look like under water but his eyes widened immediately. He'd seen pictures and video footage of all one hundred and thirty-five space shuttle launches since the very first in 1981 and he knew what every inch of every shuttle looked like. But to actually have part of a space shuttle below him right now!

'Wicked!' he mouthed before twisting around to see the same look of amazement on the others' faces.

Bob's voice suddenly boomed in Michael's earpiece.

'Great job, guys! As you can see, today we have a mock-up of a space shuttle cargo bay. It's floating approximately fifteen metres below you in a tank containing twenty-eight million litres of water. An exact replica of the Atlantis shuttle cargo bay, it measures eighteen point three metres long by four point six metres wide.'

Wow! This thing would be able to fit in a whole fleet of Tom Hill's Bugattis or give Darren Fletcher enough space to imagine he was taking a penalty at Stamford Bridge!

'Once you give me the OK, I'm gonna get you down to the shuttle and then the divers will adjust your weights to make you neutrally buoyant. Now, who can tell me what neutrally buoyant means?' asked Bob.

A voice answered immediately. Michael recognised it as Buddy, one of the four Americans here. They'd only known each other for two days, but Michael was already hoping that Buddy would become a friend. Short, with dark hair and an evil sense of humour, Buddy was one of those boys who could get away with anything. This was impressive. Michael's teacher, Mrs Jarvis, seemed to have eyes in the back of her head. The moment he tried to do something he shouldn't, he'd hear her parrot voice shout his name and she'd wave her spindly finger at his chair.

'Neutral buoyancy is the equal tendency of an object to sink or float,' recited Buddy with a drawl that made Michael picture cowboy films. 'If a combination of weights and floats are used to make an item neutrally buoyant, it will seem to almost hover under the water. This makes moving even heavy objects easy, just like it is in space.'

'Great job, Buddy,' said Bob. 'Right, are you guys ready to begin?'

Goose bumps immediately erupted over Michael's arms and neck. He lifted his right thumb up to answer Bob. This was one of the pools where American astronauts trained for space walks. They had to put in between seven and ten hours of training for each hour they were going to spend outside their spacecraft. It was the closest thing to weightlessness that you could get and he was just about to experience it! The other children all gave a 'thumbs up' and the hoist supporting them carried on its descent to the shuttle.

Michael kept looking down as they went deeper and deeper and apart from the sound of his breathing, there was silence. It's not deep water, he thought. It's just a nice warm bath. There's nothing to worry about. He knew that the water had been heated to something like twenty-eight degrees Celsius to protect the divers, and had half expected to feel the warmth of the water, but in his spacesuit the temperature stayed exactly the same. Little by little the blurry shapes below became clearer and the colossal shuttle cargo bay came into focus. There was a sudden jolt and the platform came to a halt. The divers then reappeared and busied themselves removing the barriers from the hoist and adjusting the children's weights. From the surface, Bob relayed his next instruction.

'Right, guys, we went through this yesterday in the classroom and you've all walked through it on dry land. Now it's time to see what you're made of! Michael, tell me what the "payload bay" is and what it's used for.'

Michael said nothing.

'Michael, did you hear me?'

There was silence for a few seconds more as Michael tried to order the jumble in his head. This is exactly how he felt at home, when he was asked to stand up and regurgitate the periodic table!

'Er...a "payload" is another name for cargo or goods that are being delivered or transported,' he said in a rush. 'The "payload bay" is where these goods, like satellites or lab equipment, are carried.'

'Excellent, Michael!' shouted Bob. 'Perfect! Now, Tilly, what is the "space arm" and what does it do?'

A confident, high-pitched American voice answered.

'A "space arm" is the remote manipulator arm on a shuttle. It's a kind of robotic arm, used to lift payload out of or into the cargo bay.'

'Good job, Tilly!' said Bob. 'You guys really know your stuff! So, y'all understand that you each have three tasks to perform. First, you need to locate the satellite and use the space arm to pick it up. Then you must manoeuvre it into the cargo bay and finally you need to show me that you can close the cargo bay doors. Anyone who fails to complete all three tasks is going home. Give me a "thumbs up" if you understand and you're happy to go on.'

The word 'home' made Michael's stomach turn. He'd only just got here and had absolutely no intention of going home. Not if he could help it.

He'd wondered how Bob could possibly see them fifteen metres down in the pool, until he noticed that one of the divers floating in front of them, was holding a video camera. So all their mistakes were going to be recorded then!

The children had partners to work with and Michael had been paired up with Will Bradley Junior. Will was the loudest in the group and a bit of a joker. Michael wasn't at all sure about him. He came from Washington D.C., but apart from that, Michael only knew two other things about him. He was a year older than Michael at fourteen and he had three older brothers. Michael just hoped that Will was as good at listening as he was at talking and could remember the briefing from the day before.

'You have two hours to complete your task and your time starts now!' instructed Bob through their earpieces.

Michael began immediately by pressing the communications button on the left side of his helmet. This gave him a separate radio channel to talk to his partner.

'Will, are you ready?'

'Sure am,' replied Will.

'Let's go and find the satellite first and then we can work out how we're going to get it into position for the space arm,' suggested Michael and, with a nod from Will, the two boys made a move towards the edge of the platform. Michael watched his partner's slow motion movements. It looked like Will was trying to wade through quicksand. Michael tried to jump off the platform to follow him, but toppled forwards.

'Whoa,' he shouted, trying to steady himself. 'Will, this is weird isn't it? When I move, it feels like someone's pressed the half speed button on my remote control!

Will swung around slowly.

'Yeah, it's freaky. You look just like Neil Armstrong and Buzz Aldrin did in the footage of the moon landing. D'you remember what they said?'

'Of course I do!' answered Michael, surprised at the easy

question. 'One small step for man...one giant leap for mankind!'

'No, not that! I mean the bit where Buzz Aldrin said that it took him three or four steps to get the hang of walking on the moon!'

Michael eventually managed to get a rhythm going and the two boys made their way to a thin white metal rail. This is impossible, thought Michael as he tried to wrap his glove around it. Although he could feel his fingers and move them, the pressure in his spacesuit made it so difficult to grab hold of anything tightly. This is why astronauts always look so clumsy, he thought.

'Over there! Look!' said Will suddenly as they came to the middle of the pool. When Michael looked to where Will was pointing, he saw a cluster of large, white dishes.

'They look like giant pasta bowls!' said Michael, smiling. 'I wouldn't mind having my dinner served in one of those! Let's check for the right one though. Bob said they've all got serial numbers on them.'

'Can you remember the number?' said Will, his voice telling Michael that he had absolutely no idea.

'Easy!' said Michael. 'It's the first part of my granny's telephone number...862.'

'It's not this one then,' said Will, reading the three numbers from a metal plate on the back of the first satellite dish.

'Nor this one,' said Michael, looking at a second dish nearby.

It took the boys several minutes of bobbing around like puppets before they found the right satellite.

'Got it!' shouted Michael when he saw the familiar numbers. 'Right, let's put something on it, so we can find it again.' He removed a karabiner clip with an orange tag on it from his belt and attached it to one of the metal struts of the satellite dish.

'OK, now we've got to get to the space arm and try to lift this thing up to the payload bay,' said Will, motioning for Michael to follow him.

By now, the pool was crowded. There were divers swimming around, nine other children floating in big spacesuits and a camera stuck in front of them the whole time. But to Michael, it was all strangely calm. Perhaps it was because he could hear nothing but Will. Perhaps it was because he could only move slowly in his cumbersome spacesuit…or perhaps it was because, for the first time, he knew what he was doing.

'I can't breathe!' rasped a tiny, wobbly voice suddenly in Michael's other ear.

'What was that?' said Michael, swinging around as fast as his suit would allow.

'Someone must have pressed the emergency radio button to get hold of Bob on the surface. That's the only way we'd be able to hear anyone else,' said Will.

It sounded like Aiko's voice, but Michael couldn't be sure and he couldn't see her anywhere near him.

'Aiko, this is Bob,' came a familiar drawl over the radio. 'Now I want you to listen to me. You must have your umbilical caught on something and it's stopping the flow of oxygen to your helmet. Put up your hand and stay exactly where you are and one of my guys will be with you straight away.'

'But I can't breathe... Help me!' pleaded the frantic voice.

Michael looked above and below him and turned around three hundred and sixty degrees as fast as he could, before he saw blurred shapes thrashing about back over by the satellites.

'Hold on, Aiko!' shouted Michael, pressing his emergency radio button and pushing off with his left foot in her direction. What he'd read about space walking was completely true, he thought as he tried to get some momentum going. It was as though his brain was working at full speed, but his body could only operate at half speed in his spacesuit.

'Come on, legs!'

In three or four kangaroo-type hops, Michael was close enough to see that someone else had beaten him to it and he stopped. It took him a moment to realise. Whoever it was, wasn't helping Aiko. They were moving away! There were no support divers in sight and Aiko was now floating limply on her side. Michael toppled forwards again, trying to keep his balance. He wrapped his glove around her arm and shook it, looking through her visor. Her eyes were closed.

'Wake up, Aiko! It's me, Michael. Tell me what to do!'

'Look around her, Michael,' directed Bob's calm voice over his radio. 'There will be an umbilical coming out of the back of her spacesuit, just below her waist. Make sure it's still connected and then follow it up as far as you can to see if it's caught or twisted. My divers will be with you any second, but it sounds like we don't have much time!'

Michael hesitated. What should he do? Why had he got himself involved? What if he couldn't help her?

He grabbed her and spun her around as fast as he could to see if the oxygen tube had become detached.

'Bob, the tube is in, OK.'

Michael grasped Aiko's oxygen tube as tightly as he could and gently pulled himself up on it. Up and up he went. He wasn't sure how far he'd gone before he found it.

'I've got it! The tube's caught on one of the ladders on the outside of the shuttle. It must have twisted as Aiko went down deeper.'

With a quick flick, Michael released the tube from the ladder and unwound the twisted section. He looked beneath him to see if there was any response from Aiko, but there was nothing. By now, the divers had reached her and were kicking as fast as they could to take her up to the surface. They passed Michael, who couldn't do anything other than stare and then disappeared above him.

'Don't worry, Michael,' came Bob's voice. 'You tried your best. Just leave Aiko to us now.'

But how could he not worry. If this sort of thing could happen in a pool, with people all around, what could happen tens of thousands of miles away in space? And who had he seen swimming away from Aiko instead of helping?

After what seemed like an age of just floating there and thinking about what had just happened, Michael suddenly heard Bob's voice.

'It's OK, Michael. Aiko's back with us. She just passed

out but she's fine now, thanks to you. But you need to get on. You can't afford to lose any more time.'

Michael blinked away the wetness in his eyes and made his way back to Will. Suddenly, all the things he was used to worrying about at school and at home seemed really unimportant.

'Well done, Mike,' said Will, giving his partner a pat on the back. 'It looked like Aiko was a goner!'

Michael usually hated anyone calling him Mike. At home, he would pinch his little sister, Millie, if she ever called him that. He hated it even more when Darren Fletcher and some of the others at school teased him about his love of space, by calling him 'Micky Moon'. But when Will called him Mike, there was something different about it. Will didn't know about any of the other stuff and it sounded OK.

'D'you remember what Bob said about the space arm?' asked Will, as he and Michael moved off again.

'Er...it'll be attached to one of the ports on the outside of the shuttle body,' said Michael, pointing ahead of them. 'But this time, instead of using panel switches and the shuttle computer to move the arm electronically, we've got to use hand controllers.'

'That's going to be the tricky bit,' replied Will. 'I didn't do very well in training. I'm not into video games or stuff like that and I was garbage with the controls.'

'Don't worry,' said Michael, nudging Will's shoulder. 'I've played tons of games on all sorts of machines. I'll move the arm and you get down to the satellite and make sure I get hold of it properly. OK?'

When the boys reached the shuttle their heads were level with its underside.

'Looks like the belly of some huge white whale!' said Will, lifting his arm up to touch it.

'Amazing!' was all that came from Michael's mouth as he looked up. For as long as he could remember, he'd loved looking at pictures and models of space shuttles. It didn't matter which bit of the shuttle he was looking at. He loved it all! For his ninth birthday he'd got the best present ever from his Auntie Joyce and Uncle Malcolm – a plastic click model of the Challenger space shuttle. The following birthday came a model of the Enterprise, which took him and his uncle the whole day and evening to glue together. Columbia and Discovery shuttles followed and for his last birthday, he'd received a scale model of the Atlantis shuttle, complete with balsa wood frame, tissue paper covering, model cement, white glue and a modelling knife. This kit was a professional one though, so he needed some help building it. Perhaps now that things had changed at home, his dad would have time to finish it with him.

Will's voice suddenly interrupted Michael's daydream.

'Come on, buddy. Let's get on! We have to find the port with the space arm attached to it. You go that way,' he said pointing to the left, 'and I'll go this way. Shout if you find it!'

They moved apart and started scanning the underside of the shuttle, trying to see where the space arm had been attached. The diver with the camera was right next to him as he was doing this, and Michael noticed that the clock on the top of the camera read 1:20.

'Will?' he called, his voice wavering. 'We've only got forty minutes left to complete this or we fail. We've got to find the space arm...and fast!'

Chapter Two

'Hey, Mike. What kind of saddle do you put on a space horse?' said Will from somewhere above him.

'I've no idea and I don't really care!' replied Michael. Why was Will telling jokes at a time like this? They had forty minutes left to find the space arm, get the satellite into the cargo bay and close the doors or it was all over for them!

'A saddle-lite!' announced Will, laughing so much that he almost lost his balance. 'Get it? A saddle-lite!'

'Yes, I get it. Very funny. You're a real comedian aren't you,' Michael said. You'd get on really well with Adam in my class. He's always telling lame jokes too!'

'Well, are you coming up here or not?' came back Will's relaxed voice. 'I've got it! I'm on the top of the mid-fuselage and I've found a port. Get up here as fast as you can and let's get this sucker moving!'

Michael's hands were shaking. He couldn't wait to operate the space arm. He knew he'd done well in training and just wanted to get on with it now. As he reached the top of the mid-fuselage he saw the arm, connected by one end to what he thought looked like the fuel flap on a car.

'It's huge!' he said to Will, who was looking down to see how far away the satellite dish was.

'Yeah, Carrie said it's longer than one of your weird English double-decker buses and heavier than five space shuttle crew!' Will laughed, pulling Michael's suit to move him closer. 'Look, there's the satellite,' he said pointing below them. 'You get inside and find out whether we're on a one or two hand controller manoeuvre. Let me know when you're good to go and I'll tell you which way to move.'

'OK, but you have to be facing the same way as me, so we get our lefts and rights right. I don't want you getting in a muddle, like you did in training.'

Will laughed, but Michael knew he was right. The day before, a space-mission specialist called Callie Granger had taken them for a session on robotics. It was brilliant – just like playing *Alien Capture* or *Monster Massacre* on his computer at home. The only difference was that the training screen had a picture of the shuttle cockpit on it. Michael had managed to move the space arm properly, using both computer switches and hand controllers. He'd used a mouse to click switches, which in turn moved the space arm. After that, the next stage had been to use first one, then two hand controllers, to move the arm.

Will, on the other hand, had made a complete mess of his attempt and didn't even complete the session.

He'd better get this right, thought Michael. This is too important for someone to ruin.

Will made his way down to find their satellite, whilst Michael slid from the mid-fuselage into the cargo bay. He knew from what he'd read, that the cargo bay would be big, but this was something else! He could probably fit most of his school inside! At each end were two mock-ups of the shuttle cockpit complete with hand controllers. Tilly and Buddy and Matthaeus and Liam were already sitting at two of the workstations and seemed to be right in the middle of their manoeuvres. Even Jamie, who was now on his own since Aiko's accident, was there.

'Will, are you at the satellite yet?' asked Michael. 'The others are already here, so we must be way behind time!'

'Yep,' came back Will's voice. 'I can see your karabiner clip. When you're ready, Mike, just move the arm as far as you can to the right and then down slowly. I'll tell you when to stop.'

'All right,' said Michael, struggling to wrap his gloved hands around the controllers.

'Stay calm. This is just like a game of *Robot Warfare*,' he said under his breath. Michael's right hand started to push the controller to the right. There was no sound at all and the only clue that told him he was anywhere near their target, was Will's encouraging voice.

'Mike, you've got about thirty seconds before the arm comes over my head and then you'll have to lower it using your left controller.'

Michael counted in his head. At school, even thirty seconds until the bell rang, felt like forever in Mrs Jarvis's class, but he'd only just started counting when Will screamed at him.

'Mike, stop the arm. You're going past me!'

Michael's hands opened and jumped back from the controllers.

'No!' shouted Will. 'Keep hold of them! Otherwise the arm's going to start moving back again!'

Michael took a deep breath and grabbed hold of the controllers again, waiting for Will's next command. It was like that stupid 'pin-the-tail-on-the-donkey' party game his sister liked playing. Impossible!

'OK, now move the right controller to the left until I tell you to stop,' instructed Will.

Michael slowly pushed the controller to the left.

'Stop right there,' shouted Will and Michael held the controller where it was. 'Now push the left controller forwards, until I tell you to stop.'

Michael had no idea what was happening outside the cargo bay, or whether the others were having problems like him. He pushed his left controller forwards and waited. Silence. A few seconds went by before he heard Will's voice again.

'Stop! Hold it!' he ordered. Silence again. There was nothing in Will's voice to tell Michael whether the space arm had reached him or not.

Suddenly, Michael flinched to one side of his seat as he noticed something moving towards him out of the corner of his eye. It was a space arm and from its four claws, dangled a large, white, satellite dish. He looked down at his controllers. How come the space arm was moving when he wasn't doing anything with the controllers? He couldn't understand how he'd managed to get the satellite back into the cargo bay, until he saw Buddy move forwards and grab hold of it. Between them, Buddy and Tilly lowered the satellite, until it was sitting on the cargo bay floor. They quickly detached it and then pushed the space arm back out of the doors and away.

'Will, are we ready yet? We can't have long left!'

'Nearly,' came back a strained reply from Will. 'Just got to get this hook on the...got it! Mike, now pull the left controller backwards and when I say "go", move the right controller to the left. OK?'

'Well done, Will,' said Michael, gently pulling the controller in his left hand backwards.

'Now right controller left!' shouted Will. 'I'm going to follow the arm back to the cargo bay now and help you get it in.'

Michael gently pushed his right controller to the left and kept his hand steady. Within a few seconds, Will was beside him, leaning out of the cargo bay.

'Left controller forwards a bit. Right controller left a bit. Slowly now. That's it. Hold it right there,' said Will.

As Michael looked to his right, he could see their space arm come into view. It was like a monster crab claw, with at least seven joints, all moving together. In their training session, Carrie had told them that astronauts called the space arm the 'Canadarm' and that it was used for more than just loading the cargo bay. Shuttle crew used it to check the external condition of the shuttle. To do this, they would attach a tool called the 'Orbiter boom sensing system,' to it. This was a long pole with a camera and laser on it, which they would move around the outside of the shuttle to check for any damage that might have happened during launch or in space.

Michael shuddered. It's a good job Bob hadn't asked them to use the boom as well, he thought.

'Mike, I've got hold of the satellite,' said Will, half hanging out of the cargo bay doors. 'Just move it across one centimetre at a time until it's in the middle of the cargo bay and then down to the floor.' Michael did as Will asked and within a few seconds, Will was unclipping the satellite.

'Just the cargo bay doors to go and we're done. Come on, Mike, we're nearly there! We can do this!'

Michael had seen Buddy and Tilly close the starboard door and was pleased for them but Jamie was struggling with the port door. He wasn't strong enough and without Aiko, there was no way he would do it.

'Will, let's help Jamie with his door. We can just about do it before Bob opens the starboard door again for us to do,' said Michael, standing back up and walking towards Jamie.

'We haven't got time, Mike,' said Will, shaking his head at Michael's suggestion. 'And anyway, this is supposed to be a competition. There are ten of us and only three places – do the math!'

'I don't care,' said Michael, already trying to get Jamie's attention. 'The starboard door has to close last because of the latching mechanism. You can't do that door without me and Jamie will fail if we don't help him with this one.'

Michael surprised himself. Six months ago, he would have done what Will had suggested. At school he'd been geeky 'Micky Moon', obsessed with everything to do with space. He wasn't one of the school gang and it was easier if he just went along with things. If Adam Painter was organising a football game at lunchtime, Michael stood in whatever position he was told and if Darren Fletcher decided there was something in Michael's lunchbox he fancied, he usually got it. How things had changed!

The three boys knew exactly what they needed to do to close the cargo bay doors. Bob had shown them all a video clip of the last Atlantis mission and they'd used models to practice what they'd learned. The doors were hinged at each side of the mid-fuselage and made up of five segments, connected by expansion joints. On real space missions, the doors would be operated by a set of computer commands in a specific sequence. Bob had explained that shuttle crew would use keyboards to start an automatic computer programme to control the power drives to each door. The power drives would then move a sort of shaft, which turned the rotary actuators. This caused things called the 'push rod', 'bell crank' and 'link' to push the doors open. The crew would then use the reverse sequence to pull the doors closed.

Will and Jamie moved to the outside of the cargo bay and floated by one side of the port door, whilst Michael got himself to the other.

'We've got to disconnect the power drive, so we can move this baby manually,' said Will, pressing the emergency radio button on his helmet so he could talk to Jamie. 'That means removing these bolts.' He pointed to two hand-weight-sized metal rods. 'Once we've done that, we can separate the power drive from the shaft. Then we've got to insert a crank into the shaft so we can turn the thing ourselves.'

Michael looked at the fist-sized bolts. 'How are we going to do that without any tools?'

'Not a problem!' announced an unfamiliar voice. Michael turned around to see Jamie, who was holding out a spanner and a crank that looked like they'd been made for some sort of giant DIY freak.

'Where did you get those from?' asked Michael, trying

to remember if they'd been told to bring tools with them.

'Tilly and Buddy found them when they got here and gave them to me when they were done.'

'Come on then. We can't have much time left. Let's get all the bolts undone and get these doors closed,' said Michael.

Within a few minutes, the three boys had removed the bolts from both power drives and separated them from the shafts. Then they slotted in the crank, started winding it forwards and between them pulled each door closed, first the port, then starboard door. Michael had read somewhere that it took about sixty-three seconds to close the cargo bay doors automatically. They only had about that long to do it manually!

Jamie started high-fiving Will and Michael in celebration, when suddenly a voice came booming into their helmets.

'Guys, you've got less than two minutes to get to the surface before your time's up. You'd better get a move on!'

'That's going to be tight!' groaned Jamie. 'We're more than twelve metres down now, and to stop us getting decompression sickness, we've got to go up slowly!'

Will looked at Michael and Michael knew immediately what he was thinking. If only they hadn't stopped to help Jamie, they'd be back up with Bob now.

'It's no use moaning about it,' said Michael, trying to shrug his shoulders, but finding it difficult in a spacesuit. 'Let's just get to the edge of the pool, find one of the ladders and get up as soon as we can.'

Silently, Will, Michael and Jamie pushed themselves off towards the side of the pool and then edged along the wall until they found a narrow, white metal ladder that disappeared into the distance above them.

They'd all had a lecture from Bob on decompression sickness and it had really bothered Michael. One of the divers involved today had told him how sick he'd been after spending too long in the pool and then swimming to the surface too quickly. He ended up spending six hours in something called the 'hyperbaric chamber', to try to get rid of the nitrogen bubbles that had built up in his body. According to the diver this was agony and it was something Michael was desperate to avoid.

As quickly as they dared, the three boys made their ascent, and after what seemed like an age of pulling themselves up the ladder, they all bobbed to the surface like oversized table tennis balls. Bob Sturton and some of his diving team were already there, as were Tilly, Buddy, Liam, Matthaeus, Mo and Jia Li. Michael, Will and Jamie were pulled out of the pool like enormous white sacks of potatoes.

'You guys were cutting it fine,' said Bob, smiling for once.

'How long did we have?' asked Will, lifting off his helmet and shaking his thick, blond hair.

'Twenty-three seconds!'

'Plenty of time!' laughed Will, slapping Michael's back.

Michael couldn't think of anything to say. His legs couldn't support him any more and he collapsed to the floor. He pulled his fingers through his curly brown hair and rubbed his face with the palms of his hands.

'Right, guys,' said Bob, crouching down to the seated

children. 'You've got ten minutes to get out of your EMUs, have something to eat and drink and then I want to see y'all for a quick debrief with your parents before you finish for the day.'

'What are EMUs?' asked Matthaeus. 'I don't think they have these in Germany.'

'An emu is a flightless bird, Matt,' said Will. 'You must get these in Germany too?'

Michael smiled. 'Shut up Will. EMU stands for "extra-vehicular mobility units" or spacesuits for short.'

As the pool started to empty of divers and equipment, the children wriggled themselves out of their suits, like hatching chrysalises. Tilly was the smallest in their group, even though at nearly fifteen, she was the oldest, and when Jamie stood up next to her, she only just reached his shoulder. She tidied up her hair and started gabbling to Jia Li in her shrill voice about how brilliantly she and Buddy had done, whilst Will and Jamie exchanged stories with Liam about all of their near-death experiences. Michael was silent during all of this. He was still trying to believe what he had just done.

Ten minutes later they were all sitting in a large training room, up on the first floor of the Florida Space Center (FSC), waiting to hear from Bob. Behind the children sat a group of parents. Michael turned around. He swallowed hard and felt that knot in his throat again. His dad winked and held up his right thumb in approval.

'OK, you guys. Let's make this briefing brief,' said Bob, smiling at his own joke. 'This was one of the best simulations in the NBP that I have seen in the past fifteen years.

That includes all of the astronauts we've trained and those who have already been on a mission and come back here for their refresher course. We were all taken aback by how much you guys remembered from your training sessions and dry-runs and how well you worked together as a team.'

Michael smiled at Will. This loud, over-confident American boy wasn't so bad after all. In fact Will had been the perfect partner. When Michael had panicked, Will had been calm and when things had become way too serious, Will had lightened the mood with his silly jokes and comments.

'First, we're going to take a quick look at the footage of the simulation,' explained Bob, 'then I'm going to give you some details about the next part of the Children's Moon Program (CMP).'

Michael shuffled in his seat. He hated watching himself on screen. He thought he looked stupid and didn't like his curly hair or freckles. He got enough abuse about that from Darren Fletcher at school. And his mum always insisted on taking hours of footage at Christmases and birthdays and playing them back to Granny May or other members of the family. This was different though. Everyone looked the same in their EMUs and as soon as the first picture appeared on the screen, Michael couldn't look away.

Every conversation between the pairs had been recorded. There were some nervous titters at Will's joke about the space horse and then the room fell silent when Tilly and Buddy had a fierce argument about how to manoeuvre the space arm. But what really struck Michael, was how he dealt with Aiko's twisted umbilical. He couldn't believe that he was the person on the screen acting calmly and quickly.

Michael jumped as someone near him slammed a book shut. He looked to see who it was but couldn't tell. Then he heard another one slam and then another. He thought he was going mad, until he noticed that it wasn't books being slammed shut. It was clapping. His eyes darted around the room, from smile to smile. He looked down at the desk and didn't know what he should do. How embarrassing!

Once the clapping had died down, a small man wearing a suit and round glasses spoke.

'Hello, Michael-Chan,' he said, bowing his head. 'My name is Haru Morita and am father of Aiko.'

The piece of paper he was holding fluttered in his hands.

'I want to thank you for her rescue. I not forget it for eternity. You are always welcome at home with us in Japan.'

He nodded again, but Michael sensed that a nod back might not be enough.

'That's OK, Mr Morita,' replied Michael quietly, his face burning with all the attention. 'Anyone would have done the same.'

The clapping started up again and Michael looked down at the floor, his cheeks hot.

'You have done wrong,' a voice suddenly whispered beside him. It was Jia Li, the serious-faced girl from China, who had hardly spoken a word since they'd arrived two days ago.

Michael didn't really know much about her apart from

her reputation as a science genius. From what he'd heard, she'd definitely get through the CMP. She'd spent a year on China's Shenzhou programme, learning the basics of space flight, psychology and physiology and was being sponsored by the Chinese government.

'I said you have done wrong, Michael May,' she repeated. 'You should have left Aiko alone. It was nothing to do with you. If you interfere again, it will be your turn next.'

'Right, guys. Shhhh! If we can continue please,' interrupted Bob, starting up the video again.

They all watched the remaining few minutes, making notes of Bob's suggestions on how they could improve on what they did, but Michael couldn't concentrate. He just couldn't get Jia Li's words out of his head.

Bob moved to the front of the room, his face serious again.

'We had over one hundred and twenty-five thousand applications for a place on the CMP. We selected eight thousand potential candidates to see at assessment centres on every continent, where we looked at knowledge, skills and aptitude. You are the final ten and we think that you all have something special to offer. But only three of you will get through this programme. As you know, the CMP has three core modules. To make it through the programme, you must pass every test and every simulation in every module. We looked at the possibility of Aiko retaking the neutral buoyancy test, but my colleagues and I unanimously agreed that this is the end of the road for her. We can't take the risk of someone panicking like that in a real situation. I'm sorry.'

He walked over to Aiko's father, who was wiping his eyes with his handkerchief, and handed him a piece of paper. 'You should be very proud of Aiko, Mr Morita. Getting on the programme is an amazing achievement in itself. Good luck with whatever she chooses to do in life and I hope she never loses her love of space.'

The clapping started again as Aiko's father bowed and left the room.

'For those of you still here,' said Bob, 'this is just the beginning,' and he flicked up a new screen.

CMP Candidates
Liam Best – New Zealand
Will Bradley Jr. – USA
Tilly Corran – USA
Matthaeus Fischer – Germany
Muhammad Khali – Egypt
Jia Li – China
Michael May – Great Britain
Jamie Matheson – USA
Buddy Russell – USA

CMP Modules
Neutral Buoyancy Simulation
1000m Swim
Medical
400m Run
G-Force Centrifuge
Written Test
Interview

'Your next challenge will be the swim tomorrow. That gives you an afternoon and evening to recover and come back ready to go again. Well done!'

Michael fell back in his chair and closed his eyes. It didn't seem real. The boy they nicknamed 'Micky Moon' at school, because that's all he talked about, had just passed the first part of the Children's Moon Program at the Florida Space Center. That meant that he was still in with a chance of being the first child to go to the moon!

Chapter Three

'Come on, Dad. I've got five dollars resting on this and I'm not planning on paying out!'

'It's all right for you,' said Michael's dad, grimacing and poking Michael in the ribs from behind. 'You've done this kind of thing loads of times before. The last time I was on one of these, I was with your mum and I had hair!' He took a deep breath in and exhaled very slowly.

'You wimp! Just stick your hands in the air, be quiet and wait for it to start!'

Just as Michael had finished making fun of his dad, a siren sounded and the rocket they were in jolted forwards.

'Remember, Dad, you've got to keep both arms up in the air the whole time to win the bet. If you don't, I get the cash, OK?' said Michael. He smiled. After what had happened, he was glad his dad had made it to Florida. Things could have been a lot different.

'Game on. All I've got to do is sit here, whilst we ride up and up through comets, meteors and asteroids and then plunge down a drop of nearly forty degrees in the dark! What could be easier?'

As they trundled forwards Michael became aware of what was around him. In the blue neon lights up on the ceiling, he could make out stars, comets and planets; even some sort of primitive space station. Next they entered a tunnel with flashing lights. He could hear screams coming from behind him and knew immediately why. He'd seen enough films and read enough books about space simulations to know that it was all to do with the strobe lighting they were using. He'd read that by varying the speed of the strobe flash, it would give a person in a stationary object the impression of moving either forwards or backwards. The faster the flashing, the faster the impression of moving would be. And it worked!

Suddenly the blue strobe lights disappeared and their rocket entered a star field.

'Quite beautiful this,' said Michael's dad, as he gazed at the millions of white lights around him.

'Yeah, it is…right up to the point when you find out that stars are just ginormous luminous blobs of plasma held together by their own gravity! Now have you got your arms up, Dad?'

'Of course!' answered his dad, quickly letting go of the T-bar in front of him and raising both arms.

'This is where the fun begins,' shouted Michael, his insides already feeling like he'd started the rollercoaster ride.

Click. Click. Click. The rocket finally stopped climbing. For a few seconds at the top, the blue-grey line of cars seemed to hesitate. These things always did that, thought Michael. It was just to get your heart hammering at the expectation of what was about to happen. Silence. Then it started. A steep drop…a turn…another short drop…a steep climb.

The ride threw them from left to right, forwards then backwards and Michael guessed that his dad probably had his eyes clamped shut. He was such a wimp! On the last drop, Michael thought he was going to come out of his seat and almost grabbed the bar in front of him.

The final part of the ride took them through a swirling red tunnel. Michael had explained what it was supposed to be several times, but he was pretty sure his dad still didn't have a clue. It was called a 'wormhole' – a theoretical sort of tunnel in space, which could be a shortcut through space-time. Each end of the tunnel would be a separate point in space-time. But it was more like Michael had been shrunk to the size of a blood cell and was travelling though someone's veins!

'Wow,' shouted Michael as they came to a halt. 'That was awesome! Did you see the wormhole at the end, Dad?'

Michael's dad said nothing.

When the bars on their laps lifted, they climbed out of their rocket and headed for the exit.

'I don't know about awesome, Michael,' said his dad, clutching his stomach as they went through the turnstiles. 'I think I'm going be sick!'

When they emerged into the sunlight, Michael winced, the heat like a hairdryer in his face.

'Here you go,' said his dad begrudgingly, holding out his hand.

'You didn't, did you? You chicken!' Michael said, grabbing the five dollars and stuffing it into his back pocket.

'OK. Where to now?' said Michael's dad, looking down at a map, all colour absent from his face. 'We've got three hours until the parks shut, so I don't think we'll have time to do everything. What do you want to do most?'

'How about we do the Mission: Space ride first as it is

closest?

'Sounds good to me,' said his dad, suddenly looking uncomfortable and bending his legs up and down slowly.

'Is your leg all right or do you want to take a break before we carry on?'

'It's tweaking a bit, but I'm fine,' replied Michael's dad, rubbing the lower part of his right leg. 'Anyway the railroad back to the exit goes from here, so I'll get a rest while we're on it.'

'You know that we were actually only going twenty to thirty miles an hour maximum don't you?' said Michael, reading from a pocket-sized book in the carriage. 'And Space Mountain only measures about two g-force. That's only twice the g-force on earth,' he read out.

At the CMP briefing the day before, Bob Sturton had given the nine remaining children a copy of a book called *The Dynamics of Space Simulations and Thrill Rides*. It explained the physics behind the types of simulations, which were used to train astronauts. Will had looked totally disinterested, saying he couldn't be bothered to even open it, but Michael could read this kind of stuff all day. The book also de-mystified some of the illusions and effects, like strobe lighting and centrifugal force, which were used to create thrill rides around the world. His dad ought to try reading it sometime. Perhaps then he wouldn't be such a wimp! Bob had asked the children to use their afternoon to read up on the mechanics behind the rides. Some of their findings would be in the written test if he got to the end of the CMP.

Michael wondered if he'd ever get that far. At home, he

was an expert – a sort of space nerd, but here things were different. They all seemed smarter, more knowledgeable and more confident than him. Not only would he have to get through the swim somehow, but he'd also have to do something really special to stand out.

Bob also said that they might want to try a ride or two. None of them had objected to this! Will and Liam were going to try and do as many rides as they could and Michael saw them throw their books into their lockers before leaving. If only he found it that easy! Tilly had her camcorder with her, as usual, and decided to stay behind, Mo and Matthaeus had booked themselves into the best burger bar in the area, and Jia Li had disappeared somewhere. She was always disappearing.

'Here we go, Dad,' said Michael, jolting himself back to the present. 'This is our stop.'

Michael and his dad stepped onto the platform and then down the stairs towards the exit. Once out of the park, they scanned the vast sea of cars.

'See it yet, Michael?' asked his dad.

'No. Press your bleeper again and let's just wait a few minutes. They could be parked miles away.' He gazed at the tens of thousands of coloured flecks in front of them.

After a few moments, a long white limousine with blacked out windows and a registration plate that read 'FSC 4' pulled up alongside. Out stepped a short man, wearing a military-style uniform. Michael noticed immediately that this included the shiniest black shoes he had ever seen and more interestingly, a gun of some sort in a holder strapped to a black belt. Without saying a word, the driver opened one of the back doors and waited for them to get in. Michael had never been in anything like this before.

'Wicked! Hey, we've got our own fridge or something and look at that, Dad. TV screens on the back of the headrests!'

Michael knew instantaneously what was playing on them.

'Clips of all the moon missions and landings – can't get any better than that hey, Dad? I wish I'd been around to see the first one!'

'It was amazing,' said his dad quietly.

'What d'you mean?' asked Michael.

His dad smiled and pushed himself back into his armchair-type seat.

'I saw it live on television, Michael.'

'How? I'm not being rude or anything, but I didn't think you had a television until you were like ten?'

'No we didn't. Your grandpa didn't see the point. But as soon as I found out about the first moon landing, I started begging him to get one.'

'And did he?'

'No. He said it wasn't worth it so he asked his friend, Burt, if we could go over the road and watch it at his house.'

'What was it like?' asked Michael, listening to his dad, but scanning the familiar black and white scenes on the television.

'Uncle Malcolm and I sat on the floor, right at the front of the living room and didn't move the entire time. It was really special. Mind you this isn't bad is it? How many other people ever get to page their own limousine and travel from park to park in it!' he whispered. 'This is what it must be like to be a celebrity!'

'Best make the most of it then!' said Michael, opening the fridge, handing his dad a bottle of beer and helping himself to a fizzy drink.

The journey didn't take long, but it was long enough for his dad to have a nap and for Michael to carry on reading. He knew his dad was much better but he was still putting on a brave face. If it hadn't been for this trip, he would still be resting at home after his operation.

As they pulled up to the main entrance, they had a quick look at the park map.

'It's not far,' said Michael's dad, inching out of the car and stretching his legs. 'We're booked in, so all we have to do is show our passes and we should be able to go straight on.'

'Well I will,' said Michael smiling, 'but they might not let you, looking like that!'

'What's wrong with the way I look?'

'Do you really have to ask?' replied Michael, grimacing. 'It's like looking at something out of a bad Hawaiian musical, you know, the sort that Millie watches. That shirt is disgusting and those shorts should never have made it out of the factory!' he laughed. 'You are so embarrassing!'

This was the ride Michael had been looking forward to most. His book described it as "As close as you can get to blasting into space, without leaving the earth," and he thought it would give him an idea of what a space shuttle launch would feel like. His dad, on the other hand, seemed even more nervous now than he'd been waiting to go on Space Mountain.

'What's the g-force going to be on this then, Michael?' he asked, handing their passes to the man at the front of the queue.

'A bit more on this one, Dad,' said Michael, deliberately trying to wind him up. 'It's going to be about 2.5 g-force sustained and they're going to be using a multiple-arm centrifuge to give the impression of acceleration by spinning and tilting the sealed capsules we'll be in.'

'What's that in English, Michael?' asked his dad, wiping his hands on his trousers.

'It means they are going to be tilting and spinning us around at high speeds, which will make us think that we're accelerating. Space shuttles reach about 3 g-force during launch and re-entry, so it'll be just a bit lower than that,' he replied.

'Good-oh!'

'Oh and before we go on, Dad,' said Michael, 'they'll be blowing air on us as we go round.'

'Why, has the air-conditioning broken?'

'No, it's to help avoid motion sickness.' Michael laughed at his dad's panic. 'If it gets too much for you, they put sick bags in the centrifuges a few months after it opened!'

'Hey, now what are you two lightweights doing on a serious ride like this?' said a familiar voice suddenly from behind.

Michael spun round to see Buddy Russell and his mum grinning at them. Buddy was medium height, skinny, with jet-black hair gelled up just at the front. His mum on the other hand, couldn't have looked more different. She had bleached blonde hair like Michael's mum, but was a head taller and much broader.

Buddy caught both Michael and his dad looking at them. 'Yeah, I know. I take after my dad of course!' he said.

'So you decided to do the rides too then,' said Michael shaking Buddy's hand.

'Dad, this is Buddy Russell and his mum. Buddy and Mrs Russell, this is my dad, Tim.'

'I've heard a lot about you, Buddy; all good mind. I know you made Michael's first day at the FSC a bit easier for him, so thanks.'

'You're welcome,' said Buddy in the American drawl Michael loved. 'He's not so bad.' He laughed, slapping Michael so hard on the back that he nearly fell over.

'It says here, that the capsules take four, so shall we go on together?'

Buddy, his mum Carlie, Michael and his dad, were ushered to one of the ten capsules.

'I'm not sure about this, guys,' said Carlie, lowering herself onto one of the capsule seats and pulling down the shoulder restraint. 'Are you sure I'm gonna like it?'

The two boys had engineered it so that their parents would sit next to each other and so would they.

'Hey, Mike. What d'you call a crazy moon?' whispered Buddy as the ride music started up.

'Crikey. What is it with you and Will,' said Michael, slapping his forehead. 'Did you both swallow a book of space jokes or something? I don't know – what do you call a crazy moon?'

'A Luna-tick! Ha ha. Awesome isn't it!' giggled Buddy.

Michael didn't have chance to tell Buddy, that apart from Adam Painter's rubbish football jokes, it was the lamest joke he had ever heard, because they suddenly started to move.

Over a loudspeaker, a voice told them that they were about to take part in a training session for the first manned mission to Mars. They were all trainees at a fictional place called the International Space Training Centre (ISTC) and each of the four people on the capsule would have their own job to do on board. Buddy was quick to choose the role of commander, which would mean he would be in charge of the rocket's first stage separation. Michael volunteered to be the pilot of their rocket, which they named 'The Dude' and the two parents were the engineers.

'Right you two,' said Buddy to his mum and Michael's dad, 'you're in charge of navigating us to Mars. Once we have lift off, you need to get us a slingshot around the moon for a gravity-assisted boost and then get us down onto the surface of Mars. OK?'

'What in the name of all that is holy is a "slingshot," Bud?' asked his mum.

'Mike, give her the low down on the slingshot will you,' said Buddy, who was already pressing a series of buttons around the cockpit.

'Er...how do I explain it?' said Michael stuttering and trying to think how to make a complicated subject like "gravity assisted trajectories" simple. 'Basically, a gravitational slingshot is where a spacecraft uses the movement and gravity of a planet to alter its speed and path. All planets have magnetic pull, so if a spacecraft comes close enough and at the right angle, it can use the pull of that planet to accelerate it and change its path,' finished Michael, pleased that he'd been able to regurgitate what he'd learned.

'How wonderful,' said Carlie smiling and nodding at Michael.

He didn't say anything but he knew she hadn't understood a word.

'But why would you want to risk being pulled into another planet's gravitational force, just to gain extra speed?' asked Michael's dad.

'Take this simulation, Dad,' said Michael, delighted that he was teaching his dad something for a change, 'our mission is to get to Mars. If this was real life, it would take the best part of a year to get there and to get to some of the outer planets would take decades. So, we're going to use a gravitational slingshot around the moon, to speed up the time it takes to get there, reduce the fuel used and save money.'

'Oh. I see,' said his dad, sounding impressed at Michael's description.

Michael was worried about his dad. He'd been unusually quiet. Even though it'd been eleven weeks since the operation on his leg, Michael knew that he was still recovering and often in pain.

'I'm fine,' said his dad quietly, replying to the look on his face. 'I'm just rubbish on things that go round and round. That's why I'm holding one of these!' he said, holding up a small white paper bag.

'Good luck, team,' said one of the mission control staff to Michael's capsule.

'And good luck to the crew of "The Dude",' said Buddy, rubbing his hands together.

The capsule began to shake as the countdown to lift off began and Carlie immediately started to make noises that, to Michael, could only have come from some sort of extra-terrestrial being.

'Shut up, Mom,' shouted Buddy.

'I can't help it. I'm scared,' whimpered Carlie. 'I wanna get off!'

'Five, four, three, two one...we have lift off,' said mission control.

'Too late, Mom. We're off!'

The five-and-a-half-minute ride seemed to fly by to Michael. First Buddy had to initiate the first-stage separation of the spacecraft. Then he had to engage the second-stage rocket. Michael's dad put the sick bag down for a few minutes when he and Carlie had to fire the rockets to get down to Mars and then everything went quiet for a few seconds when the simulated 'hyper sleep' was activated.

'Hey, Mike,' said Buddy, keeping his eyes firmly on the screen in front of him, 'this is amazing isn't it! If either of us ever get to experience this for real I'll die!'

Suddenly a warning siren went off. It was a meteor storm and Michael, as the pilot, was asked to deploy the spacecraft shields immediately. His dad and Carlie were then supposed to fire the rockets for the descent to Mars. Nothing happened.

'Dad, you're supposed to be firing the rockets. Come on,' moaned Michael. If only he could do it all himself. It would be so much easier.

'That's going to be a bit tricky,' said his dad in a peculiar, muffled voice.

Michael looked over to see that Carlie was holding the white paper bag up to his dad's mouth.

'Gross, Dad,' said Michael, feeling his cheeks burn.

The ride ended with Buddy having to assume manual control of the spacecraft after an autopilot malfunction and after a tense few seconds of the spacecraft sliding on ice towards a bottomless canyon, they came to a halt.

'Jeeps, that was rough,' said Carlie. Her face shimmered with beads of sweat and her body heaved up and down as if she'd just done a workout. 'If that's what it's like getting into space, then I'm glad my body is staying here, right on the earth where it belongs. That g-force is a thing no woman should ever have to endure!'

When the foursome emerged from the exit, the park was like a ghost town. There were just a handful of people dashing around to squeeze in one last ride before it closed.

Michael's dad looked at his watch, still pale from the ride.

'There's no point in doing anything else now is there? We might as well get out of the park.'

'All this work has given me an appetite!' said Carlie. 'Would you guys like to join us?'

Buddy smiled at Michael's look of surprise and under his breath he said, 'She always eats. She eats when she's sad, she eats when she's happy, she eats when she's hungry and she eats when she's not. It's been that way ever since my dad left.'

Michael secretly hoped his dad would say no to Carlie's offer. He wanted to talk to him about what was coming up next on the CMP and ask him more about seeing the first moon landing. He also couldn't afford to waste reading time. He needed to try to get all of these facts and figures fixed in his head before the written test. He hoped his disappointment didn't show as his dad nodded and hoped that the fast food in America would live up to its name

'Well I don't mind where we go or what we eat,' said Michael, 'as long as it has burgers and chips on the menu!'

'You mean fries!' corrected Buddy.

'Fries…chips…frites…who cares…as long as it's unhealthy and tasty!'

'And what about the fitness test tomorrow?' said Michael's dad. 'You've been so careful about what you've been eating Michael.'

'Mr May,' interrupted Buddy, his hand on Michael's shoulder. 'Bob Sturton may be a genius and know more about space than anyone, but I doubt he'll be able to tell what we had for dinner tonight when we get into the pool tomorrow!'

Just the word 'pool' was enough to create that old feeling in Michael, but he tried not to let his face show it. Going down in water in a spacesuit had been terrifying enough – but swimming! Even with all the practice, it was the same every time. The moment he felt the water on his skin and smelt the chlorine, he was there again – back in that pool. Pressure…sounds blurred, light, and dark, not knowing which way was up. What happened if he freaked out? What if this had all been for nothing and he couldn't do it?

Chapter Four

'So who can tell me what g-force is?' said Bob Sturton, from the front of the training room.

Nine hands shot up in the air.

'Jamie. Go for it,' said Bob, motioning for Jamie to join him at the front of the room.

As Jamie got up Michael realised just how tall he was. He'd noticed that Jamie was almost as tall as his dad in his spacesuit, but even without it today, he was a good twenty centimetres taller than Michael.

'Bet he didn't panic about making the height requirement to get on this programme!' muttered Michael. When Michael had first seen the advert for the CMP on the NASA website, he measured himself as 1.57m. For the next month he'd eaten, exercised and prayed that he would grow a centimetre to meet the minimum height.

Jamie took a deep breath and then in a slow, hesitant voice, started to tell the group what he knew about gravity. Black circles cupped his eyes, his hands were fidgeting inside his pockets and Michael was sure that his hair had not even seen a comb!

'G-force is an object's acceleration relative to free fall,' he said. 'It causes stresses and strains on objects which are felt as weight, particularly by humans. On earth, objects experience one g-force. This is exerted in an upwards direction by the ground, keeping the object from going into free-fall.' He paused for a second before adding, 'Oh and if you went on the Mission: SPACE ride you would have felt upwards g-force and Space Mountain would have given you downwards g-force,' he finished.

'That's great, Jamie. Spot on!' said Bob, turning to the big screen behind them. There were all sorts of diagrams with arrows and mathematical signs Michael didn't even know existed. This made Mrs Jarvis's maths homework look easy!

'This is what gravity looks like in diagrammatic form,' said Bob. 'What d'you think human tolerance of g-force depends on Will?' he asked.

Will had been scribbling something on the notepad in front of him. Michael just hoped it was something to do with gravity otherwise he was going to be in big trouble. Bob Sturton was known for hating laziness and for the volume of his angry voice!

'Umm...g-force is the speed of an object relative to the speed of falling?' answered Will. It sounded more like a question than an answer by the way his voice went up at the end of his sentence. Michael closed his eyes.

'Will, have you been listening at all?' boomed Bob. 'I asked what you thought the human tolerance of g-force depends on, not what g-force is!'

With his brown NASA uniform, shaved head and sergeant-major voice, he was quite intimidating.

'Do you know that there were over one-hundred-and-twenty-five-thousand applications for ten spaces on the CMP,' he shouted. You did exceptionally well in your essay, Will, but you only just scraped through the dry runs and simulations. If you don't pull your socks up, you'll be next off the programme! D'you get me?'

There was silence for a few seconds before a red-faced

Will spoke.

'Bob, I'm really sorry. I was daydreaming and I should've been listening. It won't happen again.'

'Michael, would you care to do the honours?' said Bob, telling him rather than asking.

'Thanks a lot, Will! You've dumped me right in it!' he hissed.

Michael got up from his seat and shuffled down the three steps from his bench to the front of the training room. He still had that familiar churning in his stomach, but he was getting more accustomed to it now. At the FSC it was something he'd had to do every day and he didn't quite feel the sense of panic he used to.

'Human tolerance of g-force depends on the size of the force, the length of time it's applied, the direction it acts, the location of application and the posture of the body,' said Michael in one breath.

'Exactly!' exclaimed Bob, giving Michael a wink as he went past.

As he sat back down, he glanced at what had got Will into trouble – the doodles on his notepad. There was a picture of Yoda standing by Luke Skywalker, who was strapped to something that looked like a space shuttle seat. The caption coming out of Yoda's mouth was 'Luke. Be safe and may the g-force be with you.'

'Will!' whispered Michael under his breath. 'Thanks a lot for putting me on the spot! What's the matter with you? You're going to get yourself kicked off the programme if you carry on like this!'

Will shrugged and Michael left it. He'd ask him later

when they were finished. Something wasn't right.

'OK. Let's leave the subject of g-force right there. It's clear that some of you know what's what and some of you need more work,' he said, looking straight at Will. 'But rest assured you will be tested on subjects such as g-force, gravitational sling-shots and weightlessness, so I hope you read up on the rides you went on yesterday.'

Michael had now read his book several times from cover to cover. He'd virtually memorised the whole lot – but then he'd have to, to stand a chance.

'Now, before we get ready for the first module of your fitness assessment, I thought you might like to see this,' said Bob, picking up a remote control.

With two presses, the lights dimmed, the screen lit up and a video started to play. It took the children a few seconds to realise what they were looking at and then Michael noticed that Mo's shoulders were going up and down. Jamie's too and Liam had his hand clamped over his mouth. Tilly was laughing so much it sounded like she was choking and Buddy's face was soon traffic-light red. The first bit of footage showed a blonde lady sitting in row of four seats, bracing herself for some kind of ride. As it started, she began to make peculiar sorts of animal noises but was stopped in her tracks by the man to her left, who started being sick into a paper bag.

Michael smiled and glanced over at Buddy, shaking his head and mouthing, 'They are so embarrassing!'

There was also footage of Tilly's Mum screaming to get off one of the roller coaster rides and Jamie's dad closing his eyes on Space Mountain. By the end of the three-minute video the whole room, including Bob and Michael, were hysterical.

'I thought you might like to see how you all got on yesterday,' said Bob, his mischievous look only lasting a few seconds. 'But now we've got to get back to the serious business of the fitness test. You'll be doing your swim after we finish here followed by your medical and then the run tomorrow morning. You all know that you must pass all three parts to go onto the final stage of the programme, which will be the written tests. Any questions before we get going?'

Tilly raised her hand. 'I have one. We're doing the thousand-metre swim in the NBP right. How many lengths is that exactly?'

'It's five, Tilly. Only five,' answered Bob.

'Yeah, it might only be five lengths, but we're going to have to do two hundred metres before we get to touch the edge of the pool,' moaned Jamie.

Michael knew from talking to him that the swim was the thing Jamie was dreading most. So was he. He and water just didn't mix. Not after what had happened. He couldn't be sure he'd even let go of the side. Then they'd find out.

After a quick briefing about the swim, the pool, the rules and the order they would go in, the children made their way down to the ground floor of the FSC.

In the changing rooms everyone was getting ready in their own way. Mo was humming as he usually did, Buddy had his head in yet another gruesome sci-fi book and Jia Li was helping Matthaeus adjust his goggles. But from Tilly's cubicle came a stream of chatter.

'Of course, this is my strongest module,' she said in her annoyingly screechy voice. 'I've been swimming since I was two and got picked for my county trials in May.'

Michael wished she'd shut up. Her confidence was unnerving him. He tried to block out her voice and concentrate on how he was going to approach his swim. He and his dad had been to Cottshill leisure centre twice a week since he found out about his place on the Children's Moon Program. His dad was treating it as physiotherapy for his leg and Michael as training for this swim. He'd worked out, that on average, he'd done thirty lengths each session, for nearly four weeks. The only problem was, the fear was still there and he'd never actually managed a thousand metres! Sometimes it took him an absolute age to even let go of the side.

'You OK, buddy?' asked Will.

'Yes, you're looking unwell,' said Matthaeus.

'Yeah…just want to get this over and done with,' answered Michael, cringing at his answer. He didn't want to do it at all.

As the children appeared poolside, the atmosphere changed. Will couldn't stop hopping from leg to leg, Tilly was swinging her arms in giant circles to warm them up and Jamie looked anxiously at the stretch of water ahead. Michael glanced up to one end of the pool where the parents were sitting and saw his dad. He stuck his thumbs up and smiled, but he didn't fool Michael. His dad was just as nervous as he was.

The NBP had been divided into four sections by floating buoys and ropes. Bob explained that Jia Li, Michael, Jamie,

Mo and Tilly would be using the first two lanes.

They would set off in staged intervals and use the first lane to swim one way and the second lane to swim back. Will, Liam, Matthaeus and Buddy would do the same in the other two lanes.

'Remember,' said Bob, holding up a clipboard, 'that this is not a timed event. All you have to do is start when I tell you and complete the thousand metres. You can tread water at any time and touch the ends of the pool to turn, but if you make contact with the edge of the pool at any other time, you will be disqualified. Any questions?'

Silence.

'OK. Then can I have Jia Li and Will at the edge of the pool please,' said Bob.

Michael thought Jamie still looked like he was going to throw up. The colour had left his face and his long, thin body was shivering, despite the heat in the hangar. Will and Jia Li, on the other hand, were already bent over, fingers gripped on the edge of the pool as if they were ready to take part in the Olympics.

'Let's hope someone drowns!' said Jia Li, turning to Michael and giving him a thin smile.

'As soon as the claxon sounds, you can get into the pool and start,' said Bob. In one hand, he was holding something that looked like an old-fashioned car horn and in the other, a loudspeaker that reminded Michael of school sports days.

Will and Jia Li were still in the same position, straining to stretch as far over the water as possible. It was going to be really warm; still twenty-eight degrees but out of their spacesuits they'd be able to feel it this time.

Suddenly the claxon sounded and with parents' voices ricocheting off the hangar walls, Will and Jia Li dived in. Will hardly made a splash and Jia Li managed to swim under the water for at least ten seconds.

Watch or don't watch? Shout or don't shout? Michael wasn't sure. It was less than the time it took him to complete three levels of *Alien Adventure* and he'd be in! He decided to run through his plan one more time. He'd worked out with his dad, that he'd be in the pool for about half an hour, which made it six minutes for each length.

'So, first length breast stroke, then back stroke...' he muttered. 'First length "planets of the inner solar system", second "planets of the outer solar system", third "the stages of g-force symptoms", fourth, "real life sling-shots", and the last, if I get there "previous missions to the moon".'

He glanced up to the pool and noticed that Will and Jia Li were neck and neck and almost at the other end of the pool already. Just a couple of minutes more and it would be his turn!

Bob brought the loudspeaker to his mouth. 'Michael, Liam, please get yourselves ready. Check your goggles, make sure you stretch and good luck.'

'Michael, relax. You can do this,' he said under his breath, trying to get his heart to stop its attempts at escaping. He tightened his goggles, pulled them down and moved to the edge of the pool.

Eventually the claxon reverberated around the hangar like a ship's horn. Michael didn't move. He couldn't. It was as if someone had put metal rods down through his legs and cemented them to the floor.

'Michael, it's Bob. Your dad's told me. It's OK. It really is. You've been in this pool before and he says you can swim the distance. Just concentrate on why you're here and what you want.'

It didn't help – what exactly had his dad said to Bob and why? Now everyone would find out. Michael lowered himself into the water. 'It's just a bath, a warm bath,' he whispered.

'Michael, the swim has started. If you don't go in the next five seconds, I will have to fail you,' shouted Bob.

What happened to the 'it's OK', thought Michael as he pushed off from the side. Straight away, the water seemed to be trying to get in. It was around his nose, his ears and his mouth. He couldn't get his breathing right. Water soon found its way into his mouth, making him gag. It was just like before. If he didn't get this under control, it was all over and just because of a stupid accident.

The four smaller inner planets, in order of distance from the Sun, are Mercury, Venus, Earth and Mars, thought Michael. Come on. Concentrate. They're also sometimes called the terrestrial planets because they are composed mainly of rock and metal.

By the time he had repeated this several times, his breathing had calmed down slightly and he felt he was doing something more like a breast stroke as opposed to an impression of a drowning octopus. All he needed to do now was to keep this rhythm going and not think about distance, time or the water.

Mercury is the closest planet to the Sun and the

smallest. Venus is a similar size to the Earth, but much drier with surface temperatures over four hundred degrees centigrade. The Earth is the only place in the solar system that supports life and has a natural satellite, called 'the Moon', he remembered.

He was about to run through the properties of Mars, when he heard shouting from the poolside. He looked up and saw his dad, clapping his huge hands like a seal. He couldn't hear what he was shouting but he knew he was willing him on. But as Michael turned back, he couldn't make sense of what he saw. The gap between him and Jia Li was closing rapidly! She'd been way ahead and now he had to decide whether to go past her or slow down and stay behind? He quickly decided that he needed to keep going as fast as he could for as long as he could. Jia Li was on her own. After all, this was a competition.

Michael finished describing the iron oxide in Mars's soil to himself, just as he reached the end of his first length. On his turn, he flipped himself over onto his back and pushed off as hard as he could. For the first time, he could see the maze of pipes, boxes and lights that made up the NBP ceiling. When he'd been training with his dad in Cottshill, they'd used the pool lights during his backstroke to work out how far down a length they were and how many metres they'd swum. He knew that seven hundred and fifty metres meant counting one hundred and eighty lights. But here, there was nothing obvious to count. So, he closed his eyes, went through his facts about the outer planets of the solar system as planned and tried not to let other thoughts invade his mind.

The four outer planets are sometimes called the "gas giants" due to their make-up and are much bigger than the terrestrial planets, he recalled. Back home, in his class, Chester Stanford was the gas giant! As he kicked his legs as hard as he could, Michael thought about the immense size of Jupiter, the ice and rock particles that made up Saturn's famous rings and Neptune, the size of seventeen Earths. He almost laughed out loud when he thought about the last outer planet, Uranus. During their school project presentation to parents a few weeks earlier, Chester Stanford had taken delight in trying to mention the planet Uranus as many times as possible in his five minutes. He and Harry Wilson had made a bet beforehand. If Chester could get it into his presentation more than ten times, he would get the pick of Harry's 'Match Play' football cards. He did. He even used the old-fashioned pronunciation of the word – 'U-ray-nus'.

Michael heard the claxon sound again. That would be for Jamie or Matthaeus, he reckoned.

Suddenly he was pushed under the surface by a bang on his head. Instead of taking in air, warm water poured into his mouth. There was another bang and down he went again. He kicked hard to bring himself back upright in the pool. But before he could, it happened again and the bang forced him back under. No! It couldn't be happening again. How could it? He just needed a breath. Just one, but he couldn't be sure which way was up! As soon as his head broke the surface of the water, he pulled himself around in the direction of the trouble. All Michael could see were arms and legs thrashing in the water, creating Jacuzzi-like bubbles.

Before he could work out what had happened, hot rods of pain stabbed his left calf.

'Arghh! Help!'

Treading water was impossible and the chlorine liquid lapped over his lips again.

'Help me!' Michael gurgled, spitting out a mouthful of water.

'What's the matter?' said a voice from behind him. 'What are you doing?'

'What am I doing? What a stupid question, Jamie. I'm nearly drowning, that's what!'

'Michael, can you calm down a bit. You're wasting energy and you're going to need it to finish the swim,' said Jamie, panting and fanning out his arms under the water.

'Finish the swim! You've got to be joking. I've got cramp in my left calf, I'm already exhausted and we're only on the second length. What planet are you living on Jamie!' shouted Michael.

'Suit yourself.' Jamie turned away.

'Wait a minute, Jamie...I'm sorry...I just don't know what to do...please help me,' said Michael, still splashing about.

Jamie turned back. 'Right then, you have to listen to me and do exactly as I say.' He sculled the water to come alongside Michael. 'You have to make sure that no matter what happens, you don't grab hold of me or we will both be disqualified. Now look at me, Michael.'

Michael looked up at Jamie and immediately stopped thrashing so violently.

'We all know that astronauts can get cramp. Why?' asked Jamie.

'Why are you asking me? You know the answer you idiot! Arghh! My leg!'

'Just humour me and answer the question,' said Jamie. 'Come on. Hurry up! If we don't get going soon, I'm going to be in trouble too!'

'Cramp usually happens for one of three reasons,' answered Michael. 'It's muscle-fatigue, low sodium or low potassium. So what?'

'And how do you deal with these?' asked Jamie.

'Stretch the muscle, eat a packet of crisps and eat a banana,' said Michael.

'OK, the last two options are out of the question because we happen to be in a gigantic pool, so stretch your calf in the water, until it feels better,' said Jamie.

Michael moved around for a few seconds, his face distorting like he was looking in a fairground house of horrors mirror. Gradually the hot rods cooled.

'OK...it's starting to feel a bit better now,' said Michael, sounding calm at last.

'Good. So you're going to follow me now and do everything I do,' said Jamie, 'and if you get into trouble again, shout. Just try to think about what you are doing this for.'

At that moment Bob's voice boomed out of the loud speaker.

'You guys had better get going or there is going to be a pile up!' he shouted. 'Mo is half a length behind you Jamie and closing!'

'Come on, Michael,' said Jamie. 'We've got to finish

this!'

Eventually, they reached their third length. Michael began to go through the five stages of g-force symptoms in his head. First you get a grey-out, where your vision loses its colours, then comes tunnel vision where you lose your peripheral vision. The next stage is a blackout where you lose your vision but still maintain consciousness. Then comes g-loc, which is where you lose consciousness and finally, somewhere above five g-force, you die, he thought.

Front crawl was the toughest. Michael could hear the sound of his heart drumming in his ear and he'd never been able to get the breathing right.

At the next turn, Michael was relieved to switch back to breaststroke. As he did, he saw that Jamie was right behind him and Mo was bringing up the rear. It was like a sort of water escort!

Michael could feel himself slowing right down now. He wasn't even sure if he was still going forwards. His arms and legs felt like they had weights strapped to them. Why couldn't he be neutrally buoyant for this? In zero gravity, this would be so easy!

Occasionally he looked to the poolside and saw his dad clapping and mouthing encouragement.

The first spacecraft to use the gravitational slingshot effect to reach another planet was the Mariner 10 probe. It used Venus's gravity on its way to being the first spacecraft to explore Mercury in 1974, he remembered. Michael tried hard to recall the other famous use of a gravitational slingshot, but other things started to force their way into his mind. What was going on at home? What were his class doing in the holidays? The end of the pool came into view. If he could just have a rest for a few moments, he'd be OK. He stretched out his arm.

'Last one, Michael. You can do it,' boomed a voice.

'Dad?'

Suddenly Michael was back in the room and pulled in his arm. As he turned for the final length, he saw his dad with the loudspeaker. 'Michael, this is it. Two hundred metres and you've done it. This is the home straight, the last leg…you're nearly there,' he shouted.

The last two hundred metres seemed to take longer than one of Mrs Jarvis's maths lessons. Every stroke hurt and his legs didn't feel like they were his any more. On his back, he started to go through the past missions to the moon. This was easy for him and he flew through the dates, the names of the shuttles, the astronauts and their discoveries.

The last mission to the moon was in December 1972 on Apollo 17, thought Michael. Gene Cernan and Jack Schmidt were on board.

He straightened his right arm to complete another backstroke and hit something hard. Not again! He pulled his legs down from the surface of the water and swivelled around. It was the end of the pool. He'd done it! He'd swum a thousand metres. He, Michael May, who hated water and had hardly done any swimming until two months ago, had done it!

'And the next mission to the moon will be on Apollo 18 with Michael May on board!' he whispered.

Chapter Five

'I've gotta tell you, that when it counts, you guys keep on delivering,' shouted Bob above the chatter, clapping and whooping around him. 'You showed remarkable determination and teamwork and you should all be proud of yourselves.'

Michael was sitting on the edge of the vast NBP, legs dangling in the water, arm around Jamie and Buddy's shoulders. He'd done it. They'd done it! Behind them stood a group of proud parents, red-faced and sweating from the heat in the hangar. This was the best moment ever and Michael allowed a smile to spread across his face.

'Mo, Buddy, Will and Liam all had good, solid swims,' Bob continued. 'Apart from getting disorientated and swimming back into Michael, you also had a great swim Jia Li and Jamie should be congratulated, not only for completing a tough challenge for him, but for helping Michael. But that's not all,' Bob said, smiling. 'I've just had it verified, that Tilly Corran has set a new national under fifteen record for the thousand-metre freestyle swim of twenty-three minutes and forty-one seconds!'

The cheers and hoots echoed in the hangar as everyone celebrated. Tilly jumped up to hug her mum, whose face was obscured by limp tissues, and everyone lined up to congratulate her. It was all right for her, thought Michael as he took his turn to pat her on the back. Swimming was easy for her. He deserved a medal just for getting in the water! Michael made his way to his dad and was enveloped in yet another abomination of a shirt. He closed his eyes and smiled.

Hang on a minute, thought Michael. There are nine of us. Nine of us did the swim, but he's only mentioned eight names. Who's missing?

'OK then, guys, let's get back to the job at hand,' said Bob, bursting Michael's thought bubble. 'I'm sorry to say that Matthaeus didn't complete the swim. We're not quite sure why at the moment. He's with the team doctor. But he seems to have had a problem with his eyes and shortly into the swim he had to call for assistance. I'm afraid that means he fails.'

What? Matthaeus had been looking forward to the swim. He'd done tons of lake swimming at home and he looked fine in the changing rooms, thought Michael.

'The rest of you have made it though the first part of the fitness test. We're going to give you a break for some lunch now, then at two thirty you need to be in the gym for your medical. Any questions?'

'I thought you were going to lamp me one when I asked you what you were doing in the pool!' said Jamie as he and Michael got dressed in the changing rooms.

'Yeah, I'm really sorry about that,' said Michael. 'I just panicked.'

'Some panic! What happened?'

'I…er…I really…'

'You don't have to tell me if you don't want to,' said Jamie.

Should he tell Jamie? Would he keep it to himself? If he was back home, it would be round his class faster than the register.

'Poor little Micky Moon. Afraid of a bit of water is he?'

He could just hear Darren Fletcher now. 'Had to get his baby sister to save him, hey?'

'It's kind of hard to explain,' said Michael, feeling that familiar dampness in the middle of his palms. 'It was just a normal day on holiday – well normal for us. Mum and Dad would usually work in the mornings and Millie and I would just mess about in the pool. We were in Cyprus that year and the water was lovely and warm – just like the NBP really. I was seven and she was three. I could swim OK but I wasn't very confident. She had her armbands on and jumped in. The only problem was, that she jumped in on top of me.'

Michael was suddenly back there. Muffled noises. Swirling water. It was in his eyes and ears and up his nose. It was seeping in everywhere.

'I didn't know which way was up and couldn't call for help. But then everything seemed so calm, almost peaceful. Apparently I stopped thrashing about and floated to the surface. That's when Millie ran for help. A few seconds more and...'

'It's OK, Michael. I get the picture. That's why it was such a big deal for you today.'

'It doesn't really matter now anyway. Bob's probably going to fail me on the swim because—'

'Come on you slow coaches,' said Will, pushing past them with his bag. 'I'll see you guys up in the restaurant. We've only got an hour before we need to be in the gym!'

Michael and Jamie went up to the restaurant in silence.

Michael pushed his blue tray along the metal counter, selecting a rectangular plastic container for his lunch. Ahead of him, Liam and Jia Li were arguing. From the bits Michael could hear, it sounded like Jia Li was trying to tell Liam what he should have for lunch. She was strange, he thought. After what she'd said about him helping Aiko, he was wary of her. And why did she have Matthaeus's goggles before the swim. Perhaps the bang on his head wasn't an accident?

'Hey, Mike, what's an astronaut's favourite part of a computer?' boomed Buddy's voice suddenly next to him.

'Sorry, Buddy, but I'm not in the mood for jokes,' he answered without stopping.

'Can I help? Are you worried about the medical?'

'No, I'm OK,' Michael said. 'I just want to have a bit of time on my own if that's all right with you.'

'Yeah, no problem, dude,' answered Buddy turning away and walking back to his seat.

Michael usually sat with the others for lunch, but the boys were all laughing. He needed quiet to think so joined his dad at one of the tables.

'What's up, Michael? I thought you'd be on cloud nine after the swim?'

Michael pushed the red pieces of pasta around his plate. 'Nothing really.'

'It doesn't look like nothing. What's bothering you?'

Michael tried to think of the right words, but they just didn't exist. Where did he start? Was it the guilt of lying on his application form about being a confident swimmer? Was it the fact that he'd only made it through the swim because Jamie helped him? It was also really hard to keep up with the superstars of the CMP like Tilly, Buddy and Jia Li. They seemed to find it all so easy. And then there were his suspicions about Jia Li. Should he say something or keep quiet? This was all too difficult.

Michael eventually slid his tray to one side and looked up. He couldn't keep still in his chair and his fingers found the frayed edge of his sweatshirt.

'I don't know what it is. I...I sort of feel guilty about being here I suppose.'

'Guilty?' repeated his dad. 'Guilty about what?'

'Well, I'm here because I love space and want to do everything I can to get there,' Michael said. 'But I wouldn't have got here in the first place without your help and I wouldn't still be here without Jamie's help. It just feels like I'm not good enough.'

'Michael, I'm not going to tell you what to do,' said his dad. 'You've got to start making some decisions on your own. All I can say is that you've worked really hard to get here, despite some tough things happening in our own family. You've made us all proud of you and I think you should feel good about yourself too. Don't forget, you helped Aiko and Jamie during the NBP simulation, when you didn't have to, so you've done your bit. Now what about you? What happens if you give up?'

Michael's dad pushed back his chair from the table and left.

No advice? No telling him what to do? That had to be a first! But what was he supposed to do? He ran his fingers through his hair and pulled back his tray to finish his pasta.

Through a mouthful of food, Michael eventually shouted across to Buddy, who was busy chatting to Tilly and Will.

'Buddy, it's a space bar isn't it! That's an astronaut's favourite part of a computer! How corny!'

Buddy smiled, nodded and held both thumbs up in the air.

An hour later, the want-to-be astronauts were in the FSC gym waiting for their medicals. Michael looked around. Will and Mo's conversation hummed in the corner, whilst in the middle of the room, Liam was lying on a blue gym mat, his arms crossed like a mummy. Jia Li was by herself, as usual. She had her earphones in again and looked as though she was talking to herself. Tilly was pouncing about as if she was in a gymnastics competition, dressed in a coordinated tracksuit with matching pink headband. Buddy was reading and Jamie was sitting on a bench rocking forwards and backwards.

The gym door suddenly burst open with a bang that reverberated around the room and everyone stopped. In with Bob Sturton came two other people, wearing the same brown NASA jumpsuit and carrying with them an array of equipment. It looked like they were about to conduct some sort of experiment. Perhaps this was nothing to do with going to the moon. Perhaps they had been tricked into being guinea pigs for a human clone experiment or for the illegal testing of new drugs!

'Good afternoon!' said one of the visitors, nodding to the children.

She was a small lady, with tight blond curls and large

round earrings, whose clothes looked completely mismatched to the rest of her appearance.

'My name is Rosalind Branton and I am one of the NASA doctors and space physiotherapists. My job is make sure that our astronauts are what we call "flight-fit" and that they all have a tailored fitness plan for their zero-gravity time. This is my colleague, Jim Peters, who shares this role with me,' she said, pointing to an equally small man to her left with grey hair and an expressionless face. 'Our job today is going to be to check that you meet the health requirements set out in your joining instructions and to assess whether you are fit to continue training with us, should you get through the CMP.'

Michael's mouth was dry. Were the others feeling like this? It had only been a couple of months since he'd applied for a place on the CMP. He'd passed all the tests at the initial assessment centre back home but that had been easy. Height, weight, problem solving, and an essay on 'space travel and moon exploration of the future'. But everyone had passed those tests. What was going to make him one of the final three here?

'So, before you go to do your run, Jim and I need to get some measurements from you. Tilly, Will, Michael and Mo stay here with me. I'm going to do your height, weight and lung function test. Buddy, Jamie, Liam and Jia Li you go with Jim, who will do your eye test, blood test and ECG,' she said.

'Nobody said anything about taking blood!' squeaked Tilly to Michael. 'And what on earth is an ECG when it's at home?'

'I guess they are just checking we don't have any deadly, contagious diseases!' said Will, laughing at Tilly's panic.

'And isn't an ECG one of those heart monitor things they put on old people?' said Michael, not sure he'd got it right.

'Just in case any of you are wondering why we are doing so many tests,' Rosalind said, looking over at Tilly in particular, 'these are to rule out any major health reasons, which would prevent you going into space. None of you currently wear glasses but we need to check that your eyes are healthy, particularly when they're going to be subjected to pressure during take-off and the peculiarities of zero-gravity. Your height is also important. You need to be one metre fifty-eight centimetres tall to be able to safely use our shuttle seat harnesses and reach all of the controls and equipment you will be using for your research. Now let me ask you a question...' She looked at the serious-faced children in front of her. 'Why do you think we do a blood test and what is an ECG?'

Jamie's hand shot up. Rosalind nodded at him to answer.

'I guess a blood test is needed to rule out any virus or infection that could lead to an astronaut being ill in space and an ECG or electrocardiogram is a kinda way of looking at heart function to determine any abnormalities or weaknesses,' he answered.

'Well done Jamie,' Rosalind said. 'That's exactly it. NASA cannot risk sending an astronaut on a mission if there is any chance they may become unwell and need medical attention. So we are going to look at your blood, lungs, eyes and heart now and then see what your general level of fitness is like with the run.'

The children were split into their two groups. Buddy, Jamie, Liam and Jia Li followed Jim to the far side of the room, where Bob had set up their equipment, whilst Michael, Tilly, Will and Mo waited with Rosalind.

'OK, Tilly Corran first,' said Rosalind, looking down at her clipboard. Tilly sprung forwards. She had to stand with her back to the wall whilst Rosalind shone a beam of red light from her head to her toes.

Wow, thought Michael. What an amazing machine! Having one of those would have saved Adam and him hours walking around the Andoverford High School, measuring areas and perimeters!

Another twenty seconds and all three heights had been recorded. The digital scales were next. Michael punched the air when he saw that he was two kilos lighter than he'd been in June. Will, on the other hand, was much heavier than he looked. The display showed sixty-five kilos.

'What exactly did you have to eat at lunchtime?' said Tilly laughing. 'Whole water melons!'

'Sorry, Will, could you please step off the scales. I think there has been a malfunction,' Rosalind said, frowning. Will smiled and got off as Rosalind reset them. 'OK, let's try again.'

Will stepped back on and the second reading was identical to the first.

'OK, well, Will, you're a just a lot heavier than you look,' said Rosalind, noting down Will's weight on her form. 'That's not a problem. We just need to know the weight of everything that goes on the shuttle.'

As she turned her back to check the equipment for the lung function test, Will whispered to Michael. 'Hey, look at this!'

Will started to pull his tracksuit bottoms down.

'What are you doing, Will?' hissed Michael. 'Stop messing around or you're going to get us both into trouble!'

Will grinned and carried on until he revealed plastic bags tied to each side of his boxer shorts. He showed Michael and Tilly that they each contained three small hand weights he'd found in the gym.

'I'm usually about fifty kilos without these babies!'

'Will, you are just so funny,' said Tilly in that annoying voice.

But Michael couldn't see the funny side. There was something very unfunny going on with Will and he wanted to know what.

For the lung function test, Rosalind produced two machines. One was called a 'spirometer' and looked like a miniature karaoke machine and the other was called a 'pulse Oximeter' which Michael recognised immediately from his dad's time in hospital.

'OK, guys. This is what we're going to do,' Rosalind explained. 'First we're gonna get you to use the spirometer. We're looking to see how much air you can breathe in and out and then how fast you can blow air out. Then I am gonna ask you to put the pulse Oximeter on your forefinger. There is a sensor in the clip, which will use the light of two different wavelengths to measure the level of oxygen in your blood. Any questions?'

Tilly, Mo, Michael and Will said nothing and were called, in turn, to breathe into the spirometer; first as hard as they could and then for as long as they could.

The spirometer then spewed out their results, which Rosalind clipped to their other statistics. Then it was onto the pulse Oximeter where their results were also logged.

Once the other group had finished with Jim, it was time to swap over. The eye test would be a doddle, thought Michael. Whenever Millie had one at home, his mum would drag him along too. Millie had had glasses since she was five but, so far, Michael had avoided them.

'A F R C B,' he read quickly as Jim held up a printed sign about four metres away from him. 'S P R E O R L.'

Tilly hesitated when the letters became really small and stomped back to the others when she'd finished. 'Stupid eye test! The light in here is garbage.'

After that they all had to put their chins on a rest whilst Jim took pictures of the back of their eyes.

'They'll be taking them out to look at them next,' said Will, crossing his eyes as Jim tried to look at them.

Mo was the first in their group to have his ECG. Michael and Tilly watched closely as he lay on a trolley whilst Jim stuck blue pads to his chest, sides and ankles. Colour-coded wires were then clipped onto the pads on one end and fed into the monitor at the other end. Jim asked Mo to stay still for two minutes, before his results could be logged. This was then repeated for Michael, Will and Tilly. As Michael lay there, trying to relax, all he could think of was how close he was to getting through the CMP, so by the time his two minutes were up, he was convinced that his results would show an abnormally fast heart rate.

'So, am I going to live?' asked Will as they finished. Jim said nothing and Will's grin immediately evaporated when he saw Jim get three needles out of his case.

'Tilly Corran, please sit here and pull back the sleeve on your left arm,' said Jim, without any trace of emotion. Tilly hesitated, cupping her hand over her mouth.

At last – something she's not good at, thought Michael. She looked petrified.

'It's OK, Tilly,' Michael said, 'just this last thing and you're done.'

'I...I can't...I hate needles and the sight of blood. I just can't,' squeaked Tilly. 'I didn't know we were going to have to do this. I can't do it. You go, Michael. Just leave me!'

Jim nodded to Michael, so he sat down, rolled up his sleeve and let Jim take a sample. He did the same with Will and Mo and then they all looked at Tilly. She looked close to fainting. Her petite body was shaking and her forehead was a sheen of sweat.

'Look, Tills,' said Will, lightening the mood, 'if Mike and I hold your hand, do you think you could do it? You don't want to let this small thing ruin your chances of getting up close and personal with the stars do you?'

Tilly took another few seconds before either Michael or Will knew which way she was going to go.

'Let's get it over with then,' said Tilly nodding to Jim. She sat down, rolled up her sleeve and grabbed both Michael and Will's hands. Jim worked quickly, but just as he had started to fill the vial, Tilly suddenly lurched to one side and then collapsed forwards like a sack of potatoes.

'Grab her before she hits the deck!' Will shouted to Michael as he tried to stop Tilly's head hitting the ground. All three of them ended up in a heap of limbs on the wooden floor around her. She was only unconscious for a few seconds and was livid when she came to.

'Oh my God…I can't believe I just did that! How embarrassing.' Her embarrassment then turned to panic. 'Did you get enough blood?' she snapped, as she saw Jim putting the vials of blood back in his case.

'I don't know,' replied Jim, not even looking at Tilly. 'I'll have to wait until I get back to the lab. You'll find out tomorrow.'

Once both groups had finished Rosalind called them together.

'Well done to everyone,' she said, clapping her hands. 'It's not easy to be poked and prodded but hopefully you all understand how important it is for our astronauts to be fit and healthy. I'll be back tomorrow morning with your results but, in the meantime, I'll pass you back to Bob. Bye for now.'

As Rosalind and Jim left the room, Michael took a swig of water from his bottle and tried forget about his results. There was nothing he could do about them now. But, he *could* do something about Jia Li. He'd talk to Bob later and tell him what he knew. Then he had to focus on the run. He needed to shave two seconds off his fastest time just to stay on the CMP.

Chapter Six

'Mike, are you sure you want to do this?' whispered Will, as the doors to the hotel lift slid apart.

'No, not really,' replied Michael. He looked up and down the corridor. 'But Bob didn't exactly give me a choice, did he? He said that unless I had some concrete proof that Jia Li was doing something wrong, I should just concentrate on what I was doing and leave her alone!'

'Well, he's got a point I guess...but I think it's awesome that you've got the guts to break into her room. I didn't think you had it in you buddy!' said Will. He slapped Michael on the back and rubbed his hands together in excitement.

'I don't think it's exactly breaking in if we've been given a key card,' said Michael, his face disagreeing with what he'd just said.

'Yeah, but only because I came out with that brilliant story about Jia Li being unwell and wanting to go and check on her!'

This suddenly didn't feel right at all and Michael's stomach flipped over and over.

The ten children on the CMP all had rooms on one corridor in this Florida hotel, just a few minutes from the FSC. There were doubles for those with a parent and singles for Will and Jia Li. Michael had been forced to listen to his dad's horrendous snoring for the past few nights, but he'd secretly enjoyed having him there. What would his dad think about him breaking into Jia Li's room?

Will rapped his knuckles on the door to room 326.

No answer.

A second knock. No answer.

'Perhaps I was wrong,' whispered Michael. He had his back against the wall next to the door and was scanning up and down the brightly lit corridor.

'Just stop panicking, dude,' said Will in an annoyingly calm voice. 'Look, you said you saw someone swimming away from Aiko when she was in trouble and then Jia Li warned you off during the debrief. Bizarrely, she banged into you during the swim and we have no idea why Matthaeus is out. If there's any chance she's got something to do with it, we have to find out don't we?' Will didn't wait for Michael's answer. He swiped the plastic card down through a slit on the side of the door. The red light underneath turned green. He grabbed the handle, pulled it down, and slowly pushed it open.

'Come on, Michael – quickly!' said Will. He grabbed the sleeve of Michael's sweatshirt and yanked him in.

This was nothing like his hotel room, thought Michael. For a start, it was perfectly tidy. The bed was made, there were no clothes lying on the floor, and even the shoes were paired up and in rows.

'What are we looking for exactly?' asked Will.

'Anything unusual,' answered Michael. 'If we think Jia Li is responsible for what happened to Aiko or Matthaeus, we've got to find proof!' His eyes darted around the room. Tilting his head he read out the titles of the books lined up on the desk. *The basics of Astrophysics*, *The Physiology of Space Travel*, and *Chinese Deep Space Tracking Network*.

'What's a "deep space tracking network", asked Will, flicking through the pile of magazines on Jia Li's bedside table.

'I think it's something to do with tracking asteroids and using explosives to push them away from a collision course with the earth. I don't think it's going to give us any clues though,' answered Michael.

'Hey, look, Mike. I've found her MP3 player,' said Will. 'She's always listening to this thing. D'you think Chinese music is any good?' He wiped the earphones and put them in his own ears.

All Michael could find, that was out of the ordinary, was a tub of something called 'Mentholated, petroleum-based gel'. He unscrewed the lid and the waft of minty perfume took him right back to the time he'd stayed at his Granny May's house when he'd been off school with a cough. She'd brought out a tub of stuff that smelt exactly like this and had forced him to have it rubbed on his chest. As far as he could remember, it'd had made his eyes run and had done nothing to stop his coughing! Why did Jia Li have something like this anyway? He hadn't noticed her coughing at all.

'Hey, Mike,' said Will, waving his arm for Michael to go over. 'I think I've got something. Listen to this.'

Michael took one of the earphones, wiped it, and pushed it into his ear.

He couldn't understand a word. He guessed it was Chinese, but it could have been any language really. It was a man's voice, but apart from that, Michael had no idea whether he was listening to a weather report or an assassination plot!

'Keep listening,' said Will.

There was another minute of chatter and then he heard it. Michael took the earpiece out and looked at Will.

'Told you,' said Will. 'What d'you think?'

'Er...I don't know. It doesn't prove anything...does it?'

'I think it does!' said Will. First you hear Aiko's name, then Matthaeus's, then Liam's, and finally yours. Aiko went out first, then Matthaeus and no one really knows how or why. If, I'm right, Liam will be next...and then you, buddy.'

Michael's stomach fluttered. If Will was right, he'd better warn Liam and if anything happened to Liam, he'd have to go back to Bob.

'Let's just check in the bathroom before we go,' said Will. 'Come on. She might be back soon and I wouldn't want to be here for that!'

Michael found a box, containing small, square sachets of liquid.

'What d'you reckon these are for?' asked Michael, reading the back of the box.

'No idea,' said Will, 'but it says something about bowel movements, so maybe it's to unblock you, if you get my meaning? Do you think she's taken these, to clear herself out so she'll be able to run faster!'

Michael gave a half-laugh. 'Well if they work, I could do with taking some!'

'Come on. Let's get out of here,' said Will.

The boys left the bathroom and Will was about to open the door when Michael heard a scratching sound on the other side.

'She coming in!' he hissed. 'Quick, let's get in here.' He pulled open the wardrobe door and pushed Will inside.

They closed the door just in time to hear the click of the door lock.

'Good idea, Sherlock,' whispered Will. 'But what do we do now? She might not leave until the morning, so we're stuck!'

'We'll wait until she goes to bed, then creep out,' said Michael, not convinced of his own answer. If they stayed crouching in the wardrobe for that long, he wouldn't be able to walk, let alone run in the morning!

They couldn't make out what Jia Li was doing in the room, but when Will pressed the light button on his watch, only three minutes had passed.

Michael tried sliding down the side of the wardrobe so he was, at least sitting, but there wasn't enough room, so they both ended up squatting on their haunches. It was getting hot and Michael could tell exactly what Will had had for his lunch.

'Click.'

Michael jumped. They'd been caught. What were they going to do when she opened the door? He held his breath. Nothing.

There was another click, but further away and then silence.

'I thought we were history then,' whispered Will. 'Has she gone?'

'I think so. I think I heard the door close behind her. Shall we go? I'm not sure I can stay in here much longer anyway.'

Michael pushed his side of the wardrobe door but it stayed shut. They must have come in Will's side. He slid his hand across and pushed on Will's side.

'Will, I can't open it,' said Michael, moving his hand all over the surface of the door.

'You English lightweights…let a big strong American do the honours!' said Will in his usually over-confident way.

'I can't open it either, buddy. It must be stuck,' said Will, his voice suddenly containing a hint of panic. 'Let's give both sides a really good push. Perhaps it's stiff.'

Michael and Will pressed both sides of the wardrobe doors as hard as they dared. Nothing. They were stuck. What now? Would someone notice, or would it be time for the run when the others realized they were missing? If they had to wait that long, they'd be out of the CMP and all because he'd decided to find out if Jia Li was cheating, thought Michael.

'Hold my watch a minute,' said Will, bumping Michael's arm. 'There's a button on one side, which is the light. I want you to shine it on the crack between the doors, about half way down and I'm going to see where it's stuck.'

Silently, Michael took Will's watch and pressed the buttons, one by one, until he found the light.

'Not in my face!' said Will, wincing at the brightness. 'Down there…'

Michael pressed the button and held the light out in front of him.

'No! It can't be!'

'What's the matter?' asked Michael, dreading Will's reply. How could things be worse than being stuck in a wardrobe in someone else's room, when they should be resting ready for a make-or-break run.

'It's locked,' said Will. 'That first click we heard must have been Jia Li locking the wardrobe. The second was her closing the room door.'

Michael could hear the slight panic in Will's voice. It wasn't something he'd heard before, but it matched his own. Locked. What now?

'OK, Will, my mobile is back in my room, but you've got yours haven't you?' Michael could almost feel Will's silence in the dark.

'It's in my room, charging.'

'OK then, I guess we shout until someone hears us and if Jia Li comes back, we'll have to confront her,' said Michael. 'Who's next door?'

'I think it's Buddy, but he's probably engrossed in one of his vile sci-fi books!'

Hammering on the back of the wardrobe, nearest to Buddy's wall, Will and Michael shouted. This wasn't a 'shouting at a local football match for your team' type of shout, this was a 'shouting like your lives depended on it' shout! Sweat was tickling down Michael's back. His face burned with the heat and with Will's mouth inches from his head, he thought there was a real chance that his eardrums might burst. He could hear Will panting and knew that they could only keep this up in short bursts.

After several dark minutes, they stopped.

'I can't breathe properly,' said Will. 'I just need to close my eyes for a minute.'

'There's not enough air in here,' said Michael. 'You rest

and I'll carry on, then we'll swap over.'

Michael wasn't sure whether he'd fallen asleep or passed out, but he suddenly felt someone blowing on his face. Maybe he was dreaming? The air was lovely and cool and he took great big gulps of it.

'I don't even want to ask what you two are doing together in a small wardrobe,' said a grinning Buddy.

'What happened?' asked Michael, wincing at the daylight.

'I was trying to sleep and could hear all this banging. I went down to reception to complain and the manager came up to have a word with Jia Li. When she didn't answer, he let himself in. We heard someone banging and shouting and I recognized Will's voice.'

If Michael had had the energy, he would have sprung out of the wardrobe and hugged Buddy. But all he could muster was a 'Thanks, you don't know just how much trouble we were in.'

After some feeble explanation from Will about trying to find something in the wardrobe, the manager left and the boys went next door to Buddy's.

Michael found a bottle of water on the tea and coffee tray, downed it in one go, and then fell onto Buddy's bed. Will sank into one of the chairs and closed his eyes.

'So what were you guys *really* doing in Jia Li's wardrobe?' asked Buddy, keeping his voice low.

Michael told him all about his theory, about breaking into her room and about the door on the wardrobe being locked.

'So she knows you're on to her then?' said Buddy. 'I'd be

a bit worried if I were you. She's scary.'

'You're telling me!' said Will from his chair. 'What kind of person locks someone in a small space and is happy to leave them there?'

'Do you think we should tell Bob?' said Michael, staring at the ceiling. 'I mean locking us in the wardrobe is proof that she's up to something, isn't it?

'Mmm. Maybe you ought to keep quiet,' suggested Buddy. 'You could be in a whole heap of trouble yourselves if she tells Bob that you broke into her room.'

Michael looked at his watch. It was quarter to nine. He ought to go back to his room and get some rest. He'd need it for the run tomorrow.

'Guys, I'm going to go. I'm done in and I've got a couple of things to do. Let's keep an eye on Jia Li tomorrow. If we see anything else suspicious, I'm going to speak to Bob again.'

Back in his room, Michael powered up his laptop and logged on to get his emails. There were two from his mum, asking how he was getting on, one from Millie to say she'd been in his room every day playing with whatever she fancied and a very brief one from Adam, telling him how Andoverford AFC were doing in the county cup. He suddenly had an urge to be back home. The teasing about being a space freak at school didn't seem half so bad right now, and the thought of sitting in front of the TV with his sister chattering beside him, was actually quite appealing. No judging, no tests, nothing to prove. Michael replied. He didn't tell them how he felt. He told them what he thought they'd want to know; about dangerous challenges and the fierce competition. As he typed the words, he realized for the first time how much he knew. Maybe he did deserve to be here.

The final email was from Charlotte. Michael could feel his cheeks heat up when he read that she missed him and that she was looking forward to seeing him in a few days' time, but any embarrassment evaporated when he saw her last sentence. It read, 'Thought I'd send you this so you knew. Sorry. Best just to ignore it. It's all made up. I think you're brilliant. Charlotte x.'

Michael clicked on the attachment and saw the heading 'CAR CRASH GIVES LOCAL BOY GREEN LIGHT FOR SPACE RACE'. He scanned down the page and saw that it was an article from the *Andoverford News*.

The text read, *'Local space-mad Michael May moved one stage further to his dream of being the first child astronaut after his dad was involved in a near-death car crash. "We called him Micky Moon at school, because all he talked about was stars and space," said close friend Darren Fletcher.*

"He was always daydreaming," commented class teacher Mrs. Daphne Jarvis. "But I knew from the start that there was something special about him."'

Michael hovered over the delete button. Did he want to read any more rubbish? Where did they get these lies? He could feel his cheeks flash red – this time with fury, but he carried on reading.

'Head teacher Mr. Rose said: "We're so proud of our star pupil. He wowed us with his knowledge and his project on moon exploration was exceptional. We wish Michael and his family all the best."'

'How do they get to publish this garbage?' said Michael, flicking to the last paragraph.

'But the Andoverford News can exclusively report, that life wasn't all rockets and American travel for Michael. In fact, Michael has spent most of his childhood in the care of non-family members, either in crèches or after school care whilst his parents Tim and Viv built up their own highly successful corporate careers. Even a near-drowning experience in Cyprus whilst unsupervised, didn't change life for Michael. He surrounded himself with the fantasy world of space, becoming almost obsessed with the idea of getting to the moon one day. Ironically, it was a serious car accident as his dad rushed to get to school (late for yet another parents' evening), that gave Michael his opportunity. Forced to take time off to recover, Tim May eventually recognized Michael's passion and supported his attempts to be the first child to go to the moon.

'Good luck, Michael. Everyone in Andoverford is behind you!'

All Michael could reply to Charlotte was 'Thanks. Good to know what's going on. See you soon.' He didn't know what else to write. Most of what he'd read was entirely fictional and the parts about his mum and dad, just made him squirm. How dare they say things about people they don't even know, thought Michael clicking on an icon at the bottom of the screen.

The video call-tone rang. His Granny May didn't sleep much and he knew she'd probably be up having a cup of tea, but there was no answer. He tried again. Still no answer. Time for a shower, then bed, he thought. He needed a few minutes to unwind and relax before the run tomorrow. He was just about to log off when the video call-tone sounded.

'Hi, Granny,' said Michael, as he pressed the 'accept' button. 'It's Michael. How are you?'

'I can hear you, dear, but I can't see you,' warbled the voice.

'You probably haven't turned on your camera, Granny,' said Michael. 'It's on top of the screen and the button is underneath.'

This wasn't unusual. She always forgot. In fact, she seemed to forget a lot these days.

'Just a minute, dear,' she shouted, probably thinking she had to talk louder because he couldn't see her.

The screen flickered and Granny May's face appeared.

'Ooh, Michael, you're there, dear,' she said, looking genuinely amazed at the fact she could see him. 'What time is it in America?'

'Er…it's half past nine…that means it's half past two in the morning in England. Couldn't you sleep?'

'Well you know me, Michael. It doesn't matter when I sleep. It's all the same to me. But tell me how you're getting on? Is it really hard?'

Michael could see every crevice on his granny's face and wondered how old people got to be so wrinkly. And why did they suddenly think that lilac-coloured hair was a good idea?

'Er…yes it is hard. Everyone here wants to be one of the last three on the CMP, so it's really competitive. But I'm OK and Dad seems to be enjoying himself. Wait until you see the foul shirts he bought in the shopping mall today!'

Michael heard about Millie and her new riding lessons and tried to keep up his smile, as his granny started to tell him what had happened at her last bridge game on Tuesday.

'I said to Mrs Hart…I said if you're going to cheat, you can leave my house this very minute,' she said, 'and then she started to argue with me.'

Michael's money was on his granny. He'd never known her to give up on anything; board games, cards or arguments. He'd heard that she'd even written to her local MP every day for six months, until he agreed to campaign for a speed camera to be installed on Presholm High Street.

'Look, Michael, I will let you go, my dear. You need to get your sleep for tomorrow. We're all really proud of you and I hope you make it to the very end,' she said, opening up the crevices around her mouth as she smiled.

As Michael closed down his laptop and stretched out on his bed, he thought about his Granny May's last words. Did he have what it would take to get to the end and was Jia Li going to try and stop him?

When Michael woke up the next morning, everything ached. Crouching in a wardrobe hadn't exactly been the preparation he'd been thinking of for the run. Will looked just as bad at breakfast, groaning when he got up to go to the buffet table.

'Have you seen her this morning?' whispered Michael, as he loaded up his tray with muesli, toast and fruit.

'Yep. I reckon we're on to something,' said Will. 'She asked Liam if she could sit with him for breakfast. Look.'

Michael glanced over Will's shoulder and saw Jia Li talking to Liam. That alone was suspicious. She'd hardly said a word since she arrived and now she was acting like his best friend.

'And what's going on with you, Will? You've been acting like an idiot since we got here,' said Michael.

Will shrugged and looked away.

'Are you trying to get kicked off the programme or something, because I think Bob was pretty close?' There was definitely something Will wasn't telling him...something wasn't right.

Two hours later, the children were called and made their way outside. They would be running on a track like the ones used to move the mobile launch towers and shuttles from the shuttle assembly building to the launch pad. Michael remembered that the real ones were something like thirty metres wide and over three-and-a-half-miles long. Fortunately he would only have to run a fraction of the distance, and instead of the rough stony surface of the transporter track, they would be running on exactly the same polyurethane material found on athletics tracks.

'Guys, if you'd like to do your final warm-up, we're going to get this race underway. You'll see that we've marked your lanes and that there's a lane's gap between each of you. When I call you to the starting line, you can either use the blocks we've given you, or move them out of the way. My starting command will be "On your marks, get set, go." When you hear the starting pistol fire, you're off,' he finished. 'Any questions?'

Again, there was silence as Tilly, Will, Buddy, Michael,

Mo, Liam, Jia Li and Jamie started jogging around and stretching in preparation. Michael reckoned that Buddy, Tilly and Jia Li would probably be the fastest. Although they were small, he had the impression that they were the fittest on the programme and after the swim and the blood test, he knew how determined Tilly was to win. Was he that determined?

Time was up. This is it, thought Michael. All the football, running and swimming he had done in the last few weeks would hopefully pay off. Just four hundred metres to run in under one minute and thirty seconds and he could be through to the last part of the CMP.

Everyone lined up, some choosing to use starting blocks, others like Michael deciding not to. As he looked along the length of the track, Michael decided to pretend he was running to make a shuttle launch.

He saw Bob holding the starting pistol and signalling to Jim Peters, who was standing at the four hundred metre mark. The next part seemed to happen in slow motion and Bob's voice sounded like it was coming out at half speed.

'On your marks...get set...bang.' Off went the gun and Michael rose from his starting position as fast as he could. He started to pump his arms forwards and backwards, taking big strides and pushing off the surface as quickly as he could. His dad had been on at him to stand more upright but his natural running stance was bent slightly forwards with his fingers clenched tightly. He didn't know how far he'd run but he could feel the lactic acid building up in his thigh muscles. They were on fire. He tried to ignore it, focusing on the launch pad in front of him.

Suddenly, Tilly came flying past him on his right and Buddy zoomed ahead on his left. Panic started to build up. Almost there – just keep going, he thought. Breathing was starting to hurt and his rib cage chest felt like it was being pulled apart. Come on Michael! How badly do you really want this?

It was all over. He'd crossed the line and by the time he'd caught his breath and looked up, everyone was there. Will and Jamie were lying on the floor panting, Liam was clutching his thighs and Tilly, Mo and Buddy were doing high fives. Only Jia Li looked like she'd hardly done anything, her earphones already back in.

So had he been fast enough? Was he through to the final stage of the CMP or was it all over?

Chapter Seven

'Just two more days to go and we'll find out whether we need to get you measured up for a new Andoverford High School uniform or NASA overalls! It sounds strange doesn't it?' said Michael's dad.

There was no reply. Michael picked up another stone from the sand and threw it at a small rock protruding from the sea. His eyes needed matchsticks to hold them up, like one of those Tom and Jerry scenes. He didn't want to talk. He didn't want to do anything. His body ached and his mind was full.

They had the morning off before the final simulation, so Michael's dad had suggested driving to the coast – just the two of them. He'd tried to start up several conversations in the car but each time all that Michael could manage was a monosyllabic answer. A few minutes after they'd set off Michael's head flopped back onto the headrest. By the time he woke up they were already parked up at the beach.

'Shall we get an ice cream?' Michael's dad said, breaking the silence again.

'If you want. I'm not bothered.'

'Come on, Michael,' said his dad. 'The day you turn down the chance of a rum and raisin ice cream is the day that the earth stops spinning. D'you want to talk about it?'

'Not really, Dad. I'm just tired,' replied Michael, still mulling over the email Charlotte had sent him. 'Can we just spend a couple of hours without talking about space, or the CMP or about passing or failing please?' he asked.

'Of course,' said his dad, getting up from the sand and brushing himself off. 'Let's walk down to the arcade and have a go on the slot machines. We can pretend we're in Las Vegas!'

'Well you're dressed for the part at least!' said Michael, raising his eyebrows and shaking his head at the fashion disaster in front of him.

They changed ten dollars each into quarters and within twenty minutes had fed their coins to the rows of hungry slot machines. While his dad was getting excited about a dollar win on the one-armed bandit, Michael spent most of his time rolling his quarters down a metal slot and onto a platform full of coins. As the platform moved forwards and backwards it created a pile of coins right on the edge.

'Just one more,' Michael said to himself, as he let his last quarter roll down the slope 'and the whole lot's mine!'

Unfortunately, the machine somehow managed to add his last coin to the pile on the edge and Michael's game was over.

'Stupid machine!' was all that Michael could think to say when his last coin was kidnapped. 'This game's for mugs anyway! It's just chance.'

He looked around for his dad but he was nowhere to be seen. He could hear a lot of shouting and whooping by the arcade entrance, so made his way though a sea of T-shirt and shorts to find out what was happening. There were people crowding round one of the slot machines. He couldn't see who was on the machine, but the voice was unmistakable.

'Come on then, baby! Show me what you've got!'

Michael managed to squeeze through the group of mainly teenage boys to see what was going on. There was his dad, in another of his Hawaiian shirts, stomach protruding, talking to a machine, stroking it and getting more excited than Michael had ever seen him before.

'Hey, Michael. This is for the big one! Three hundred bucks are resting on the last pull,' he shouted. 'D'you want to do it?'

'Er...no...you're OK, Dad,' Michael said, stepping back into the crowd. 'Why don't you. It looks like you're enjoying yourself!'

As his dad put his hand on the lever, the crowd started a low hum, which sounded like a performance car engine. It then rose to the pitch of a 1500cc motorbike, before eventually reaching the sound of something between a 50cc scooter and a mosquito. Michael's dad pulled the lever down and a blur of fruit symbols spun round. It seemed to take forever for the fruit to settle in their positions. He thought his dad was on to win the ten-dollar prize for three cherries but they clicked past one by one. When the machine eventually stopped the crowd went wild. Michael was caught in the middle of high-fives and whoops and total strangers were patting his dad on the back.

'Your dad's just won the jackpot!' said a lanky teenager, with several body piercings and tattoos.

By the time Michael could get a clear view of the three hundred dollar signs in a row, the machine was playing a trumpet fanfare and spewing out the winnings in plastic dollar chips.

Michael smiled as he watched his dad stuffing the chips

into his shorts' pockets as fast as he could.

'Not bad is it hey, Michael!' said his dad, as the two of them walked back to the car, twisting their waffle cones round and round, to lick the melting ice cream. 'We're walking along the beach in Florida's glorious sunshine, eating ice cream together. Can't think of anything much better than this, can you?'

'No,' answered Michael, the corners of his mouth quivering.

'What's the matter?' asked his dad.

It built up inside him and suddenly and he couldn't keep it in any longer. He didn't have time to move his ice cream out of the way and it sprayed everywhere. He just had to laugh and then couldn't stop; a laugh that made his stomach hurt and his face red; a laugh that could easily turn into tears.

'Oh…sorry, Dad,' Michael said, in a Tilly-type voice.

'What's so funny?'

'Well, from my point of view, I'm walking along the beach in Florida, with a dad who, not only is wearing the most embarrassing, awful and old-fashioned clothes ever, he's also got dollar bills bulging out of his pockets, a sun burnt head and raspberry ripple ice cream running down his chin! What could be more perfect!'

By the time Michael and his dad returned to the FSC, there was an hour and a half until the g-force centrifuge simulation. Michael knew there was nothing he could do to prepare for it, so he joined the others in the common room whilst his dad went out shopping for souvenirs. His mum had asked for a new mobile phone as they were cheaper in America and Millie had begged for a stupid bright pink Minnie Mouse cap. The only decent souvenir Michael could think of would be a letter to say that he'd been chosen as one of the final three and was going to be trained as the first child astronaut! He'd swap all the rubbish in the shops for that.

Tilly was playing with her camcorder in the corner, Will and Buddy were telling each other jokes and Jamie was on the phone. Michael guessed from the tone of his voice that something was wrong. When Jamie had finished he slumped into one of the comfy chairs and picked up a book. Michael sat down next to him and picked up a magazine from the reading pile. What should he say? Should he ask? Michael's question must have been written on his face, because Jamie answered, unprompted.

'It's my mom. She's ill. She has good nights and bad nights and this was one of the bad ones. Her nurse had to call an ambulance and Dad had to go home.'

'Sorry,' Michael said. That was what people had said to him when they found out about his dad's car crash. It hadn't really helped, but what else was there to say?

'That's OK,' Jamie replied, still looking at his book. 'There's nothing any of us can do. Dad's with her now and she's stable.'

'How come you're here?'

'Like most of you guys, I've always loved everything to do with space. My mom and dad used to take me and my brother over to the Kennedy Space Center most weekends when we were small' he said, 'and then Mom got sick...really sick. We ended up selling our house to pay for her treatment. Dad started a night job to try and pay off some of our debts and we stopped doing anything that cost money.'

'Oh...er...I'm sorry,' said Michael. 'I...'

'It's OK,' said Jamie, interrupting. 'No one ever knows what to say when I tell them, so I don't tell many people...and I don't want anyone else here to know. I can't bear the looks of sympathy.'

Michael nodded. What else should he say? He couldn't remember a time when his room hadn't been full of gadgets and games and toys. He also couldn't remember a single year when he hadn't been on at least two trips abroad. Although Jamie towered above Michael with his sporty physique, blond hair and piercing blue eyes, he suddenly looked small.

'My dad saw an article in the local paper about this programme and told me about it. He thinks I'm doing it because I love space and want a chance to go to the moon, but I'm also doing it for what we can all get out of it,' said Jamie quietly. 'I found out that if I get through, we get somewhere to live and my mum can use the living expenses money for her next lot of treatment. If I don't make it, I can't bear to think what'll happen.'

Michael noticed the two rivulets trickle down Jamie's cheeks and pulled his chair in closer.

'So how did you end up applying to get on the CMP?' said Jamie, sniffing and wiping his nose on the sleeve of his jumper.

'Oh, it was fluke really,' answered Michael. 'My teacher

chose "space" as our end of year class project and that landed me on the NASA website. I mean, I'm always on the NASA website looking up stuff but that's when I saw the advert about this programme. Then my dad had a car crash – a really bad one, so I gave up thinking about it.'

He thought back to the day of his dad's accident. He'd been at the after school club, waiting for his dad to turn up for parents' evening. As the minutes ticked by and his dad was late, he was livid. His parents always did this kind of thing. They were so wrapped up in their work that he and Millie always seemed to come last. School had eventually called his mum and just after she'd arrived the phone call came through about the crash. He'd never seen his mum in pieces like that and it had really scared him. But strangely, the accident changed everything. His dad had to be off work for three months and that gave Michael chance to spend time with him – proper time. They had built models together, played computer games, but above all, his dad had put together a training programme to get him ready for the CMP assessment centre. Without the accident he wouldn't have made it here.

Michael had only read the first few pages of his 'Space Exploration' magazine when Bob Sturton arrived for the simulation. He asked them all to put on their skin-tight anti-g suits, which led to hysterical laughter.

'Jamie, you look like a bean pole!' laughed Will.

It was true, thought Michael. Jamie's legs looked even longer and skinnier (if that was possible!).

'Well, at least I'm not stumbling around like I'm consti-pated!' replied Jamie, pointing at Will's pigeon-toed walk.

Michael now understood why these anti-g suits were sometimes called 'second skins'!

'OK, guys. As you know, this is your last physical test and simulation. We're going to be seeing how you tolerate acceleration and gravity far above what you experience on earth. You're going to take turns in the centrifuge, where we're going to simulate the g-force experienced on shuttle take-off and maybe a bit more,' Bob explained.

Michael's could feel his heart beat in his head and when he looked to his left, Liam was clutching his stomach.

'Are you OK?' mouthed Michael.

Liam didn't say anything. He pointed his finger into his mouth and held his stomach again.

'So why have we got you in these ridiculous-looking suits?' Bob asked.

Jia Li's hand went straight up.

'Jia Li?'

'These anti-g suits are designed to prevent black-out and g-loc which happen when blood drains from the brain and pools in the lower part of the body under acceleration,' she answered quickly.

'Exactly! And what are the symptoms of hypoxia?' asked Bob, looking to the others.

Michael knew the five stages of g-force symptoms by heart. Going through them is what had seen him through the fourth length of the NBP swim. He stuck his hand up but before he could say anything, Jia Li butted in.

'Grey out, tunnel vision, blackout, loss of consciousness (g-loc) and then death,' she said, not even acknowledging Michael.

'Thank you, Jia Li. We just need to make sure you can withstand a shuttle launch. If we start to see any of these signs, we'll stop the simulation,' said Bob.

Michael knew that shuttle launches and re-entry were about three gs; less than some of the roller coaster rides in Florida and far less than the five or six gs that formula one racing car drivers had to cope with. This should be just like having another ride on Mission: Space.

'Your anti-g suits are all fitted with something called "bladders,"' explained Bob. 'Can anyone tell me what they are?'

'Is it some kind of bottle that collects your urine if you want to pee on take off?' answered Will, smiling at his answer.

Bob's face and neck instantaneously turned red and Michael was expecting him to explode at Will. Instead, Bob completely ignored him and answered the question himself.

'These bladders are inflated by air under pressure and they then press firmly on your abdomen and legs, helping to restrict the draining of blood away from the brain. They'll feel peculiar but without them, you'll feel worse. Trust me!'

Bob continued to talk to the children about how they were going to carry out the simulation. He would call them one at a time into the centrifuge room. They would be strapped in the same type of seat as used on space shuttles and would be in the same perpendicular position. Their bladders would be inflated and then the simulation would begin. He told them, much to Michael's relief, that the simulation should last no more than a minute or so.

The human centrifuge was in a separate building, next to the NBP. As Michael and the others walked outside, the running track disappeared into the distance ahead of him. On the horizon, he imagined the site of the shuttle launch pad and an image of him dressed up and ready to go on his first mission to the moon flashed into his head.

'Michael, this way,' said Tilly, jolting him out of his daydream and they entered the High-g training centre.

The centrifuge room was much smaller inside than Michael had imagined. With a white circular wall, only two small doors and little porthole windows dotted around the top of the wall, it looked like something out of a sci-fi film.

'If that's the centrifuge,' said Buddy, pointing to the only object in the room, 'it looks like someone's just made it out of scrap metal and dumped it there!' He didn't sound impressed.

'Yeah, it looks like a crane that has had two chairs attached to the ends and then been bolted to the floor,' agreed Will.

Once they'd had chance to look inside the pods, where they'd be sitting, Bob told them about the 'straining manoeuvre' which they were to use if they started to 'grey-out'. He explained that this entailed holding their breath for a few seconds, whilst tensing their abdomen muscles. Along with the anti-g suits they were wearing, this would reduce the chance of g-loc happening.

'Hey, Mike,' said Will, laughing and poking Michael in the stomach, 'better work out where your abdomen muscles are then!'

Michael forced a smile, hiding what he was really feeling. He was used to this sort of thing from Darren Fletcher at school and hated it. The last thing he needed when he was so close to getting through the CMP, was for that idiot Will to stuff things up for him by distracting him.

'Will, you're up first,' announced Bob. 'The rest of you can go up to the observation room until your turn. Your parents are already up there.'

Although he wanted to thump Will for his stupid comments, Michael wished him good luck with the others and left the room.

His dad was waiting for him up in the observation room. As Michael came in, he started to laugh. 'And you have the nerve to make fun of what I wear!' he said pointing to the tight anti-g suit Michael was wearing.

Michael smiled, but said nothing. He was too concerned about what was about to happen in the room below.

'Hey, Michael, whilst you were having your chat downstairs, I was watching this really great video clip on the Internet,' his dad said excitedly. 'D'you know, they can get this machine up to ten gs and there's this piece of footage where this guy's eyeballs...'

'Dad!' interrupted Michael. 'I don't want to know! It's bad enough having to go on the thing, without you telling me all the horrible stuff that's happened to other people!'

'Oh. Sorry. I was just excited that's all,' he said, and quickly fumbled around for the remote control to turn off the screen.

As the sound from the computer disappeared, Michael heard a loud humming from below them. They peered out from one of the porthole windows and saw Will getting into one of the pods, helped by three or four NASA staff. As the pod door closed, Michael's stomach jumped. A few minutes and it would be his turn.

The humming noise got louder and louder until the centrifuge arms started to move. They creaked as they spun, first slowly and then building up speed.

'I can't bear to look,' said Michael's dad, lifting his hand to his mouth. 'It makes me feel sick just watching.'

Jamie, Buddy and Mo had decided not to watch but were flicking magazine pages too quickly to be reading them. Tilly was speaking into her camcorder again and Liam and Jia Li had disappeared. Where had she taken him and what was she up to now? Michael was the only one who watched. He had no idea how fast the arm was spinning or how Will was feeling inside but it looked like he'd been grabbed by robot and was being shaken to death!

Suddenly, after what had seemed to Michael like just a few seconds, the arm slowed down and came to halt. The NASA staff appeared like a swarm of bees to release Will but, before he left the pod, it looked like he was being checked over by Rosalind Branton, the doctor who'd done their medicals. As Will climbed out, Michael noticed that his near-permanent grin had gone and that he was unsteady on his feet. A speaker in the observation room then called for Tilly to go down to the centrifuge.

'Good luck, Tills,' said Buddy.

'Just remember to hold your breath and pull in your stomach,' Michael reminded her.

Without a word, Tilly adjusted her tracksuit top, hugged

her mum who was already crying, and left the room.

'She's not as brave as she looks,' sniffled Tilly's mum, a petite lady, who reminded Michael of a small mouse. 'She's only doing this to get her name in the papers and to get on television.'

Michael shrugged at what Tilly's mum had said. He had no idea what she meant and wasn't about to ask.

'She wants to be an actress,' Tilly's mum continued, even though Michael wasn't interested. 'I mean she's brilliant at swimming and good at school, but her dream is to be a Hollywood actress. She just saw the advert for this programme and decided that if she got through, she would be famous and then could do what she wanted. She's already got her own reality programme on TV when she finishes here.'

'She never said anything about that,' said Michael, suddenly getting the point of the camcorder.

'Would you? I mean she doesn't want any of the official people knowing in case it jeopardises her chances.' Tilly's mum suddenly looked worried and moved in closer to Michael. 'You won't say anything, will you?' she whispered.

'Er...no,' Michael said, more abruptly than he meant. 'It doesn't make any difference why she's here, but I doubt she'll be able to use any of her footage afterwards. We had to sign that confidentiality form when we got here. We all want one of those three spaces, Mrs Corran, and we're all going to do whatever we can to get one.'

Saying the words suddenly made it all clear. The geeky space freak at home wasn't geeky here. He knew his stuff, he was fit and there was no reason why he shouldn't be one of the three chosen!

He heard the centrifuge start up again and suggested a game of cards. It reminded Michael of the 'Match Play' games that Chester Stanford and Harry Wilson tried to have under the desks at school. That all seemed an eternity ago, but right now he wouldn't mind being in one of Mrs Jarvis's boring maths classes!

They'd barely finished one game, when Jamie's name was called. Without really thinking about it, Michael jumped to his feet, gave him a hug and wished him good luck. The room seemed quite empty now. There was just Michael, Mo and Buddy to go. Michael's dad was watching the news channel on the computer in the corner and Buddy's mum was on her second bag of crisps...or chips.

'Mom, fancy doing this simulation for me?' joked Buddy.

'Jeeps, if you think you're gonna get me on something like that after the ride we did the other day, you've got to have a screw loose! I've got my own g-force thing going on moving myself. Why would I put myself through that!' she said.

Michael knew that Buddy was worried about his mum. Since his dad left, her eating had spiralled out of control and she was just getting bigger and bigger. Every time Buddy tried to mention it, she just laughed it off and told him not to worry.

Liam was next and it only seemed like a minute or two before a speaker on the wall requested, 'Michael May, please come down to the high g-force centrifuge room.'

'Good luck, Mike!' said Buddy's mum through a

mouthful of crisps.

'Yeah sock it to them, Michael!' added his dad, grabbing him for a quick hug. 'Remember, breathe, abdomen, concentrate.'

Michael's mouth immediately felt dry and his head was suddenly full of cotton wool. His legs weren't responding and he wasn't sure he could even get downstairs.

'Michael!' said his dad. 'Come on. You can do it. Just sit there, breathe properly and you'll be fine.'

Michael breathed in as far as he could and on the outbreath whispered, 'Believe. Focus. Do it!' He'd seen it on poster of Buzz Aldrin at the National Space Museum, which was now hanging on his bedroom wall. He repeated it over and over again until he got into the centrifuge room.

'Right, Michael,' said Bob, unaware of Michael's wobble. 'You know the drill. We are going to pump up your bladder with air, adjust your seat to fit you, strap you in and then it's all systems go. I'm going to be in radio contact with you the whole way, through your headset. If you feel strange at any time, let me know and we'll get you out of there. Any questions?'

Michael shook his head. He wasn't really sure if he had any questions but his mouth wouldn't work. There was also the most horrible smell in the room. Several brown jumpsuits suddenly engulfed him and within seconds, he was strapped into his seat and his anti-g suit inflated with air. It felt like someone was squeezing his stomach and legs at the same time. It didn't hurt but felt odd. Once he'd been secured, Bob closed the pod door. Michael's skin immediately started to feel clammy. His heart was at full speed and he had the urge to reach forward and open the door. He tried to breathe more deeply, but could only take short breaths.

'Michael. This is Bob. Can you hear me?'

Michael said nothing. He was still panting and couldn't speak. What was happening?

'Michael. This is Bob. Take your time. Try to breathe slowly – in through your nose and out through your mouth. We won't start until you're ready,' he said.

Slowly, Michael's heart seemed to return to something like near normal and he was able to take longer breaths.

'Sorry, Bob,' he managed. 'I'm not sure what happened then.'

'Michael. No need to worry. That was just a minor panic attack. Lots of people get them. It's quite normal and if you can get yourself out of one, that's good news,' said Bob. 'Just let me know when you're good to go and we'll begin.'

Chapter Eight

Michael had been told that there would be a camera inside the pod, so rather than speak, he held up his right thumb. As soon as he did this, the humming noise started and he was off.

For the first few seconds, it didn't seem too bad. Bob was talking to him constantly, asking him if he was all right. Then there was sudden acceleration and the pod was thrown out at an angle. The pressure squashed his whole body down in his seat and he knew this must be the start of the increased g-force.

'Going up to two gs now, Michael,' Bob announced. 'Remember when I say now, I want you to hold your breath and pull your abdomen in. You got that?'

'Yes,' said Michael, trying to get his breathing under control again.

'Now!' said Bob calmly.

Michael held his breath and pulled in his stomach as tightly as he could. It felt like something was crushing him from above. His eyes ached and his head was feather-light again.

'Going up to three gs, now four gs. You OK, Michael?'

Michael nodded although he felt anything other than OK. 'Just a few seconds more,' he thought to himself. 'A few seconds more and he would have done it.'

There was suddenly a jolt and the pressure disappeared instantaneously. It felt like he was still spinning, but when the pod door opened Michael realised he had stopped completely.

'Michael. Congratulations. You just made it through shuttle launch and re-entry!' announced Bob's excited voice.

The first face he saw was the NASA space physiotherapist's.

'Hi Michael. I'm Rosalind Branton. Could you tell me your date of birth and home address please.'

Michael hesitated. Why was she asking him a stupid question? He'd just been spun around in a giant centrifuge and she was asking him about his birthday!

'Er...fourteenth of May. Morningview, Sandy Lane, Andoverford, UK,' he answered.

'Good. I'm just going to listen to your chest for a second and then I want you to read what's on this card,' she said. She held her stethoscope on Michael's chest for a few seconds and handed him a yellow card.

Slowly, Michael read out, 'Space has more to offer the earth, than anyone on the earth could imagine being able to offer space.'

Rosalind smiled at Michael and he heard her say something like 'Bob, roger this exercise.' He couldn't be completely sure, but it sounded like he'd made it through!

'Mum? Hi it's me,' said Michael, counting forwards five hours to work out what time it would be in England.

'Michael! How are you? What's happening? How did you get on with your g-force thingy?' asked his mum like a machine gun.

'Yes, I'm fine thanks. Dad and I are about to go down for

breakfast but I just thought I'd phone and let you and Millie know that I got through the g-force simulation.' If only his mum could see the look on his face, she'd know how he was feeling.

Actually, it was his dad's idea to call home, but Michael was already glad he'd suggested it. He pulled the phone away from his ear just in time to stop the shriek from bursting his eardrum. His dad started to laugh next to him.

'Brilliant! Oh well done, Michael. I'm so proud of you…how many of the others made it through?' she asked.

'I'm not really sure. Liam bombed out though. He said he had bad stomach cramps before we started but they still made him do it. He had diarrhoea this morning and then threw up and passed out on the centrifuge just before he got to three gs. Bob Sturton, the guy who's running the programme, is going to see us in an hour and give us our fitness results. I can't believe that we're finally going to find out who is through to the final stage!'

'Oh well, if he's out and everyone else got through, there are only seven of you left, so you've almost got a fifty per cent chance of being in the final three! That's brilliant!' she shouted.

Michael didn't want to ruin his mum's excitement, so he left out the bit about the possibility that he could still have failed the run.

'Yeah, I'm really pleased, Mum. And how are you and Millie?'

'We're fine, Michael. Millie's at holiday club this morning and I'm working from home. I've got a business proposal to write but I should be done by mid afternoon, so Millie and I are going shopping and then to see some girlie film at the cinema. You'd hate it. It's full of princesses and ponies!'

'Yeah, I don't feel like I'm missing out,' said Michael, pulling a face at his dad.

A few months ago, Michael would never have had this sort of conversation with his mum. It would have all been about schoolwork and her work and what he should and shouldn't be doing, but since his dad's car accident, things had changed – for the better. He'd had all that time at the hospital to talk to her and she'd been around much more at home. His dad now had three months off work and his mum was trying hard to reduce her hours and spend more time with him and Millie.

'Well look, you go and have your pancakes or whatever they call breakfast over there and call me when you've more news,' said his mum. 'Can I just have a quick word with your dad please?'

Michael passed the phone to his dad and signalled that he was going to go downstairs to the hotel restaurant to wait for him. There was absolutely no need to hear his dad get all soppy with his mum. Too embarrassing!

As he walked into the restaurant, Michael noticed that Liam, Buddy and his mum were already there. Should he go over and say hello or just get his breakfast and sit on the opposite side of the room? That would be the easy option. How would Liam be feeling after yesterday and what should he say to him?

As he stopped at their cluttered table to say good morning, Michael noticed the enormous plates of breakfast in front of Buddy and his mum. It looked like they'd tipped several cooked breakfasts onto each plate. There was a small mountain of streaky bacon, a handful of sausages, scrambled eggs, waffles, mushrooms, tomatoes and fried bread, all smothered with a sticky, glistening sauce, which Michael had discovered was maple syrup. It looked amazing!

'Hi, Liam,' said Michael, trying to sound sympathetic. 'How are you?'

'Hey, Mike, I'm good thanks,' said Liam, looking anything other than good. He looked the colour of candle wax and had the same sort of shine to his skin. 'Buddy and his mum are comfort eating for me after yesterday,' he said, pointing at their plates. 'I couldn't eat anything last night after throwing my guts up on that machine, and I can't face it this morning either!'

'Yes, thanks for that,' said Michael. 'I was on the centrifuge after you and the stench was evil!'

'Yeah, thought I'd leave a little something for you!'

'Are you coming to get your fitness test results this morning?' Michael asked, half-knowing what the answer would be.

'No point, man,' Liam answered. 'I had a chat with Bob last night and I'm done on the programme. I passed all the fitness tests but apparently, if you pass out or vomit during the g-force simulation, you're out too. Can't have that happening on take-off can you?'

'Not even if you felt ill before you went on?' asked Michael.

'Nah. I suddenly got these cramps after we had our

food, but what can I do? It's over.'

'Did you eat anything different yesterday?' asked Michael, unable to get the list of names on Jia Li's MP3 player out of his head.

'Don't think so, why? Jia Li just got me the same as she was having.'

'Jia Li?'

'Yeah, she got my food for me.'

Now why would Jia Li, who had been silent for most of the CMP, suddenly offer to help Liam? Was it possible? Could she have had something to do with Liam being sick? If she had, then according to her list he would be next, thought Michael. Perhaps it was time to go back to Bob.

Liam was being very matter-of-fact about things but Michael noticed the look on his face. It was anything other than matter-of-fact.

'Well I'm sorry for you, Liam,' said Michael, patting him on the back. 'I mean I'm sorry you're not going to get to live out your dream.'

'Don't worry, Mike. You've still got a chance. Just promise me you'll keep going. You deserve it more than anyone, well, apart from me of course.' He laughed. 'No seriously, you're not a show-off like Jia Li, who thinks she is owed a place and I can see you just love all that,' he said, pointing up at the roof.

'Let's keep in touch,' said Michael. 'Bob has all my details and if you want to, I'll get yours?'

'Sure thing,' nodded Liam. 'We can email and photo mail and I've got this really wicked game we can play over the net!'

After they had said their goodbyes, Michael and his dad sat down for their breakfasts.

'I'm ready for a Buddy-sized breakfast,' said Michael with a mouthful of sausage, 'and I can eat whatever I like without worrying about running or swimming or being swung round and round in small circles!'

'Welcome back, for the last day of the Children's Moon Program,' said Bob Sturton as the remaining children and parents gathered in the training room. 'Before we go any further, I just want to say huge congratulations to you all for getting this far. I have been constantly impressed by your knowledge, your determination and your skills and you should all be very proud of yourselves.' He looked around at every nervous face in the room. 'As you know, we had to say goodbye to Liam Best yesterday. G-force simulations are never easy and there is not a lot you can do if the effects of acceleration make you ill. We wish him well in whatever he goes on to do in life and I'm betting we won't see the last of him!'

Michael shot a glance at Jia Li. Nothing. He looked across at Will, who shrugged.

'For the rest of you, I'm going to make this as quick and painless as possible,' said Bob, turning to face the wall. 'I'm going to put up your fitness results on the screen. You'll get a pass or fail for each area. If you fail anything, I'm afraid it's the end of the road for you. If you've passed, you'll sit your written test this afternoon, followed by a one to one session with me. By this evening, we should have our final three candidates for astronaut training!'

All eyes were fixed on the screen and there was silence.

Jamie Matheson
Swim – Pass
Run – 1min 24secs – Pass
Height – 1m 77cm – Pass
Blood Test – Pass
ECG – Pass
Lung Function – Pass

It didn't take more than two seconds for everyone to scan down Jamie's results and cheer in celebration. Jamie punched his fists up and down in the air. Then the next name appeared.

Will Bradley Junior
Swim – Pass
Run – 1 min 20secs – Pass
Height – 1m 62cm – Pass
Blood Test – Pass
ECG – Pass
Lung Function – Pass

Again, the room exploded into applause. Will smirked.

Tilly Corran
Swim – Pass
Run – 1min 18secs – Pass
Height – 1m 58cm – Pass

Blood Test – Fail
ECG – Pass
Lung Function – Pass

What? Michael re-read the results.

'No way!' shrieked Tilly as she saw the word 'fail' appear next to her name 'Why? How did I fail the blood test? You can't be serious. You're going to get rid of someone like me, who's your best candidate by far! You've got to be joking!

Bob tried to talk, but was hit by another battery of questions and statements from Tilly.

'I broke the national swimming record for God's sake!' she shouted. 'And I bet I was first in the run too. How can you do this?' Tilly's mum was of little help. She was crying again.

'Tilly…Tilly,' said Bob, trying to calm things down. 'Tilly, if you'll just stop shouting, I can explain. I can tell you about the blood tests now or we can meet up straight after this and I can talk to you privately. It's up to you,' he offered.

'Private! Why would I want to have a private chat? We've been watched from the moment we arrived here – twenty-four seven! I've got nothing to hide, so tell me now,' she demanded.

'OK,' agreed Bob, looking uncomfortable for the first time. 'First of all, we struggled to get a decent blood sample because you fainted but, when we analysed it, we found that you've got a vitamin B12 deficiency.'

'What do you mean I've got a vitamin B12 deficiency?

What's that anyway?' snapped Tilly, sounding desperate.

Michael had to sort of agree with what she was saying. She was clearly one of the best athletes among them, and apart from her wobble during the blood test, she'd never shown any fear or worry about the simulations or tests. In fact Michael got the impression that she enjoyed pushing herself. On the other hand, with her out, his chances had just improved again.

'You have a lack of vitamin B12 in your body,' Bob explained calmly. 'It probably explains why you were light-headed during the medical.'

'Garbage!' shouted Tilly, throwing her hands up in the air in frustration. 'That was because I can't stand the sight of blood – not because of any deficiency!'

'All right, Tilly. I take your point but even if that's true, the fact remains that you need treatment and we can't accept you onto our astronaut training programme if you need medication.'

'Well just give it to me now and be done with it!'

'I'm afraid it doesn't work like that,' said Bob. 'Your doctor will need to work out what's causing it first. It could be diet-related or maybe have something to do with how your body absorbs the vitamin. Either way, it won't be an overnight fix and we just can't wait that long to see how you respond. I'm really sorry Tilly. You've done so well.'

All of a sudden, Tilly went very quiet and very still.

This was just like his mum in the seconds before she exploded, thought Michael.

But the explosion didn't happen. Without another word, Tilly shoved her mum aside, got up, grabbed her jacket from the back of the chair and flew out of the room.

'Kind of spoilt things, hasn't it,' said Will to Michael as they waited for something to happen. 'Bob's so going to regret that last bit!'

'What d'you mean, "regret it?"' asked Michael.

'Don't tell me we've got to this stage and you haven't noticed it?' said Will tutting and shaking his head.

'Noticed what? Will you're not making any sense. What are you talking about?' Michael hated riddles and it wasn't the time for cryptic jokes.

'The camera…she—'

'Right, can we move on now please,' said Bob, pointing back at the screen.

'Tell you later,' whispered Will. 'You're not going to believe it!'

Michael scanned the screen from top to bottom. It read:

Michael May
Swim – Pass
Run – 1min 29 seconds – Pass
Height – 1m 58cm – Pass
Blood – Pass
ECG – Pass
Lung Function – Pass

'Yes…yes!' mouthed Michael, turning to find his dad. I did it! I ran four hundred metres with a second to spare!

His dad smiled and Michael knew. He might only be a few hours away from reaching the final three!

Now there was just Jia Li, Mo and Buddy to go.

No one was surprised to see Jia Li's results, including Jia Li. There was no celebration, no smile, nothing. She just nodded, put her earphones back in and left the room, before finding out whether Mo or Buddy had made it.

Michael put both hands up to his mouth, waiting for the results.

Mo started to cry when his results appeared. He'd failed the run. 'What do I say to my country,' he wept. 'They put me here. They celebrated my success and now I let them down.'

Michael had chatted to Mo a few times and knew a bit about the troubles in Egypt. Mo had become quite a celebrity there since getting a place on the CMP and he'd told Michael about the pressure he felt, representing a country being torn apart by protests and violence. Thank goodness life in Andoverford wasn't this complicated!

Now it was just Buddy. He had to make it. He and Jamie were the only two who really got Michael.

'Yeah! That's my boy,' shrieked Buddy's mum, as his results appeared on the screen. She jumped up, threw her cavernous gold bag on the floor and grabbed Buddy's arms.

It didn't take long for Will, Michael and Jamie to join her.

'And you think my dancing is embarrassing!' said Michael's dad, joining the back of their conga-style routine.

Bob let the celebrations run until everyone had collapsed back into their seats and then talked to the four boys about their final hurdle.

'You guys have made it to the last part of the CMP. Congratulations.'

These words forced the hairs on Michael's arms to stand

to attention.

'When you've had time to grab a quick drink and a snack, and I find Jia Li, we're going to crack on and do your written test. You'll have an hour to write what you like on "Space travel and moon exploration of the future" and another hour to complete the multiple-choice test. This should be a breeze for you all. You've already written a thousand words on the subject as part of your application and you clearly all know a huge amount about space.'

Michael knew that Will's essay had been brilliant, as Bob had told them all and Jia Li's was bound to be perfect, but he was still in with a chance. The way Will had been behaving lately, it was anyone's guess what he would write.

A bar of chocolate and a fizzy drink later and Michael was ready to go. All he had to do was regurgitate his own words and get them down on paper. He thought back to Mrs Glendinning at school and the hours she'd spent listening to him talk about his dream of going to the moon. Her voice was always soothing to him, so he closed his eyes, thought of her singing accent and, when Bob instructed them to start, picked up his pen. He wrote the first two words before he realised that his pen had run out of ink. Typical, he thought, digging his hand into his coat pocket for his spare. He'd had this pen for ages at school and it had to run out now! He had so much to write, he couldn't afford to waste any time. It wasn't there, but there was something very peculiar in his pocket. It felt slimy and sticky. He pulled out his hand to see that it was now black! His pocket was full of ink – but there were no refill cartridges! He looked around the room. Everyone else's heads were down, scribbling like mad.

After waving his arms around in the air like a demented octopus, Bob looked up from his desk and noticed.

'What's up?' he whispered at Michael's table.

Michael showed him his hands and told him about the pen.

'You'd better go and get cleaned up and I'll put a pen on your table Michael. Be quick though. This is your chance to shine.'

Michael pushed back his chair and made his way through the room. As he passed her, Jia Li looked up from her paper and grinned. So he'd been right all along! She was trying to get rid of her competition one by one. Well it wouldn't work with him, he thought almost running down the corridor. He'd show her! He'd show her what he was made of! Bob had said it was his chance to shine and that's what he intended to do! He'd deal with her later.

Quickly cleaning up, Michael dashed back to the room and flung himself into his seat. His idea had been to describe some of the real-life goals for future moon exploration and then to share his fantasies about what space travel and life in space could look like. All those hours of dreaming and sketching pictures in his bedroom would come in handy now.

He started writing about the plans of countries such as Japan and China to begin lunar mining as a way of discovering new energy sources. When he'd applied to get on the CMP, he hadn't thought that he might end up with someone like Jia Li on the programme. She probably knew everything he knew about Chinese plans for moon exploration – and loads more!

Then he went on to describe how India had been able to carry out chemical and mineralogical mapping of the moon's surface and their amazing discovery of water molecules in lunar soil. He wrote that Europe and Russia were also planning to send unmanned spacecraft to the moon within the next decade and that their aim was to eventually create a permanent moon base.

Now for the good bit! Michael had summoned up the courage to talk to Bob after the swim. He'd asked him exactly what the eventual winner of the CMP would be doing as part of a shuttle crew. He knew it was to help with research and experiments but found out that the Americans were also interested in mining on the moon. If he made it into space he'd be using robot technology to collect moon samples, analyse them and record the findings. It would be just like using the Canadarm all over again!

Michael checked the clock. He had twenty minutes left to get across his ideas about the future of space travel. He wrote 'Eventually, people will be able to consider space as just another tourist destination. Visits to 'space hotels' will become affordable for the average family as they fly through the earth's atmosphere on shuttle-like planes.'

Michael wanted to finish his essay with something memorable. His last words read, 'If space is infinite, so are its possibilities. What can be discovered and experienced is only limited by man's own limitations.'

The multiple-choice test was also relatively easy for

Michael. He circled answers to questions on g-force, gravitational slingshots, weightlessness and the solar system with time to spare. He couldn't have done more and he didn't think he could have done any better.

Jia Li had also finished whilst Will looked like he was doodling on the side of his paper. Buddy and Jamie were still furiously scribbling when Bob called time.

'OK, the very last thing I'm gonna ask you to do on this programme, is come and chat to me about why you want to be the first child astronaut,' said Bob. 'This should be the easiest thing of all, because it's the reason you decided to apply to get on the CMP. Michael, you're first. If you come with me into the side room, we can get this thing over.'

Michael's chair scraped as he got up and he was immediately back in Mrs Jarvis's classroom. He would love his class to see him right now. Adam would be pleased for him, Chester would probably make some silly joke and even Darren Fletcher might have something good to say about 'Micky Moon'.

Will, Jamie and Buddy all gave him a thumbs up as he left the room and Michael tried to find the energy to psyche himself up to do this one last thing.

'So, Michael, you've got ten minutes to convince me that you should be the first boy in space. Off you go,' said Bob.

Michael hesitated. This should be easy. He should be able to talk about space in his sleep but he couldn't find the right place to start.

'Er...I...er,' he mumbled

'Take your time, Michael,' said Bob. 'Just tell me how you feel first.'

'Er…I'm shocked, excited, amazed, confused and still can't believe I'm here,' he answered. 'I bet everyone will say that they've always had a love of space, but that won't be true. Not in the same way as me anyhow.'

'What do you mean?'

'The first thing I can ever remember,' said Michael 'is leaning on my windowsill, with the curtains open, staring at the blackness of the sky. Except it's not black is it. It's shades of yellow and bright white, all set out in patterns, which meant nothing to me to start with, apart from that they were meant to be there. Every time my mum came in to say goodnight, I begged her to leave my curtains open so I could look at what was out there and what might be out there. She didn't understood and I don't think she even does today, but I want to be out there amongst all of that. I want to find out if what I strained to see through my telescope is real or just imagined.'

Michael fumbled in his pocket and handed something to Bob.

Bob smiled as he looked at it.

'That's my bedroom,' Michael said proudly. 'That's where I sleep, work and spend most of my time at home. Up to now, that's as close as I've ever got to being in space. I want to make it real now,' he said quietly.

Bob looked at the slightly dog-eared photo Michael had given him. It showed shelves full of model shuttles and books on space. The walls were covered with posters depicting the solar system and its planets. His laptop and TV were covered in NASA stickers and newspaper cuttings about space missions and his whole ceiling looked like it had rocket stalactites growing down from it.

'Thanks, Michael,' said Bob.

Michael couldn't tell from Bob's face if he had said enough or whether what he'd said was any good.

'Oh just one more thing, before you go, Michael,' added Bob. 'What will do you do if you don't make it through?'

Michael didn't even need to think of an answer. It just came out.

'If I don't get through this programme, I'll just find another way of getting into space or working somewhere like this. But I just have to get through.'

'How did you do, buddy?' quizzed Will as Michael sat back down in the common room.

'Hard to say really,' admitted Michael. 'I couldn't tell from Bob's face whether I'm going to space or going home!'

Bob called Will in and after his ten minutes were up, it was Jamie's and then Buddy's turn. Eventually Jia Li reappeared and had her time with Bob.

Michael had mixed feelings. He really wanted Jamie, Will and Buddy to do well, but not at his expense.

As the boys finished their interviews with Bob they slumped one by one into their tub chairs. Jia Li left the room again.

'Hey, what were you trying to tell me about Tilly,' asked Michael.

'Oh yeah. I can't believe you haven't noticed. She's been recording as much as she can for that TV programme she'd going to be on! Her mum confided in me,' said Will.

Michael smiled, guessing that her mum had confided in several people about Tilly's plans.

'She's had a hidden camera in one of the buttons on her tracksuit top and microphones everywhere! That's why she was always talking, explaining what we were about to do. I've told Bob and she's going to be in a whole heap of trouble after signing that confidentiality agreement!'

'How long d'you think Bob will keep us in suspense?' said Jamie, looking at his watch and jigging his leg up and down.

'It won't be long, guys,' answered Will, pushing back his chair and picking up a rucksack from the floor.

'How do you know?' asked Michael, 'and why have you got that with you?' he said, pointing to Will's rucksack. 'We weren't supposed to bring anything were we?'

'Well, you didn't really think I'd make it did you?' said Will. 'The boy whose dad got him his place because of who he is? The boy who had three months of tutoring to get him up to speed for the programme? The boy who doesn't know the difference between Saturn's rings and party rings? Come on. Surely you'd sussed me out?'

Both Michael and Jamie's jaws opened slowly, but nothing came out.

Chapter Nine

'What are you talking about, dude?' said Buddy, sitting forwards and frowning.

'Don't worry. I'm not bothered. It was another hair-brained idea from my dad to get me to do something he'd be proud of,' answered Will.

'But…but Bob said your application essay was one of the best he'd ever seen,' stammered Jamie.

'Well it would be, wouldn't it,' Will replied, kicking his rucksack.

'Why?'

'It was written by one of my dad's friends, who used to work for NASA! He had to dumb it down a bit, to make it sound more like something a fourteen-year-old would write. You didn't think that was me, did you? How gullible are you guys!'

Michael didn't like the way Will's tone had changed. It sounded as if Will was blaming them for not spotting he was a fraud.

'How could you do that Will? How could you dupe us like that? You took up a place that someone who really loves space could have had! I think that stinks!' said Michael, red in the face.

'Yes well, that's me all over isn't it,' answered Will, reaching the door of the room. 'Selfish to the last!'

'So did you tell Bob, or were you found out then?' asked Jamie, who was now up on his feet, pointing his finger at Will. 'Come on. If you're just going to run off like the cheat you are, you at least owe it to us to explain what happened first.'

Will hesitated and for a moment, Michael saw something unfamiliar in his eyes. He put his rucksack down, shuffled back to his chair and folded into it. He started to tell Jamie, Michael and Buddy how he'd come to be on the CMP, how his father had disapproved of him wanting to become a professional American football player and told him that he couldn't waste an opportunity like this one.

'Didn't you tell him that you weren't interested?' asked Michael. He couldn't believe that someone as confident as Will could be forced into doing something he didn't want to. Him maybe, but not Will.

'You've never met my dad have you,' said Will. 'Of course you haven't. He was the only American parent not here! "Got to learn to stand on your own two feet some time, my boy," he said. "Don't need to come and watch you. You know what you have to do. You've had enough coaching."'

'Coaching?' Jamie asked.

'Oh yeah. Three months of coaching about stars, the moon, space and other deadly dull stuff!'

Once Will had started, he couldn't stop. He showed Jamie, Buddy and Michael a picture of his three older, very successful brothers. Jimmy was in the army, Bobby in the navy and Joe had just become the youngest person to get a job with the presidential political team.

'How am I ever going to compete with that?'

Suddenly Michael felt for Will. It had been a battle to get

his own parents to understand how important this was for him but Will must have gone through absolute hell.

'That explains why you did such stupid stuff during the programme,' said Jamie. 'Were you trying to get thrown off?'

'No…well kind of…I mean, to start with, I really didn't care. But as I got through each stage, I started to think I could actually do it. I started to enjoy the CMP and I scraped through most things. But then I had to write the essay!'

'And?'

'Well I hadn't written the first essay had I! So it was impossible to re-write something I'd never written in the first place wasn't it,' Will explained.

'So what did you tell Bob?' asked Michael, trying to imagine what had happened during their conversation in the side room.

'Well he was stuck for words and asked me why I had only written two lines of my essay!' said Will. 'I told him that I'd had second thoughts and that I didn't think this was for me. He just said he was sorry to see me go and that his report would speak very highly of me. That'll be enough to impress my dad and keep him off my back for a while so no harm done I guess! My fault for letting myself be forced into it I reckon!'

'Will, I'll say goodbye now,' said Bob, poking his head round the door. Thanks for all your hard work and the heads up about Tilly and good luck in the future. Michael, Buddy, Jamie and Jia Li, please would you come down to the training room. I've made my decision.'

Michael, Buddy and Jamie said a hurried goodbye to Will and for a moment just stood, looking at each other.

'Good luck, guys,' said Jamie.

'You too,' replied Michael.

'Jia Li. Congratulations. You're one of my final three,' said Bob, handing her a piece of paper. 'As you'll see, your test results were astounding. You passed everything and came first in the written test and simulations. It's going to be a pleasure to work with you.'

Jia Li took the paper, nodded at it and sat perfectly still.

If that was me, thought Michael, I wouldn't be sitting still; I'd be jumping up and down. What a strange reaction. If only he'd been able to prove she'd been up to something. But it was too late for that now.

'Buddy, I'm delighted to be able to offer you as place as well,' said Bob, smiling.

'Come on!' shouted Buddy, jumping up and pumping his fists up and down in the air and then checking to make sure his gelled hair was in place.

Michael and Jamie laughed. Typical Buddy!

Now things were serious. There were two of them left and only one place.

'There's nothing really between you two,' said Bob, looking down at their final CMP results. 'Jamie, you were faster in the run and stronger in the neutral buoyancy simulation, but Michael, your test and essay were exceptional.

Buddy left the room and the three of them sat down at a small table in one corner of the training room, the room where they'd spent hours of briefings and debriefs over the past week. Jamie couldn't look at Bob and sat like a giant parched sunflower, head down. Michael, on the other hand, couldn't take his eyes off Bob's face, looking for any inkling of a decision.

Come on. Get on with it. This is unbearable, he thought.

Both Dads were waiting outside like nervous wrecks. They couldn't stop pacing up and down like caged animals in a zoo. Even Michael's mum, Millie and Granny May were apparently sitting next to the phone at home, willing it to ring.

'And so, to my decision,' said Bob stroking the side of his face, swallowing hard. 'I have decided that the final place on the CMP astronaut training is to go to…Michael.'

It took a few seconds for Michael to process the words. He looked at Bob, then at Jamie and then at Bob again.

'Me?' he whispered, his voice barely audible. 'I've done it?'

'Yes, Michael,' Bob confirmed, nodding so that Michael fully understood. 'It's you!'

'But how? I never thought it would be me. Oh, Jamie, I'm sorry,' he said, suddenly remembering Jamie's mum.

Jamie looked completely devastated. The colour had escaped from his face and his eyes glistened.

'Don't worry about it, Michael. It's OK,' Jamie said. 'I'll just find another way to help Mom. This was just one idea. Congratulations. You deserve it.'

'I'm sorry, Jamie,' said Bob, holding his hand. 'Michael just tipped the scales I'm afraid. You know if I had another place...'

'It's OK, Bob. If I was to choose anyone to win, it would be Michael.'

Jamie pushed back his chair and got up slowly.

'Just do one last thing for me will you,' he asked. 'Let me go out and tell my dad myself. I think it will be better coming from me.'

Michael hadn't given a second thought to what failure would mean to Jamie and his family. They'd been given somewhere to live in Florida and money whilst Jamie was here. What would happen now? How would they survive? How would they be able to carry on paying for his mum's treatment?

Jamie disappeared and Michael heard muffled voices for a couple of minutes, then silence. Suddenly the door flew open and in stumbled his bemused-looking dad. He looked at Bob, then Michael and back to Bob, who was nodding.

'Have you...I mean...are you...Michael, you've done it!' he eventually managed to squeak.

Michael had never seen his dad so excited...about anything!

He picked Michael up with an enormous bear hug and squeezed him.

'Steady on, Dad, you're going to kill me before I even get up there!' He laughed, pointing to the ceiling.

'So this is it, Bob,' checked Michael's dad more seriously. 'Michael has won a place on the CMP astronaut training and is still in with a chance of being the first child in space?'

'Too right,' Bob said, offering his hand. 'Your son has been amazing over the past week. He's worked hard, learned quickly and never given up. That's the kind of person NASA want on board – literally!'

Michael felt sorry for Jamie but, right now, he felt like screaming, dancing, singing and crying with happiness. He'd done it. Stupid old 'head in the clouds Micky Moon' might still get to the moon!

'It's gonna take a bit of time to sink in,' said Bob as Michael and his dad stood glued to the spot, 'so I suggest we meet in the morning and I can take you through what happens next.'

Michael's dad pulled out his mobile and dialled Andoverford 311506.

'Hello.'

'Is that the May residence?' asked Michael's dad, pinching his nose and talking in a bad Scottish accent. Michael was on tiptoes with his ear against the receiver so he could hear.

'Yes,' answered Michael's mum, clearly waiting for some sort of sales pitch to follow.

'Yes. Hello. My name is Mr Aldrin. I Apollo...gise for calling you at this time in the morning but I wonder if I could have a quick chat to you about solar energy for your property and whether you could benefit from our new gravity-defying roof tiles? We're taking appointments in your area on Saturn-day if that's any good for you?'

Michael clamped his hand over his mouth to stop the laugh from escaping and heard his mum stutter on the other end.

'I'm… afraid it's not a convenient time at the moment,' she said. 'I'm waiting for an important phone call from America, so you'll have to call back.'

'Even if I'm calling from America with some really, really exciting news?' said Michael's dad in his own voice.

'Tim!' She shouted so loudly it made him pull the receiver away from his ear. 'Is that you messing around?'

'Sorry, Viv, I couldn't resist!'

'Come on. Tell me what happened. Millie and your mum are here too and the phone is on speaker.'

'Mum, hi it's Michael. I'm sorry but you're going to have to take that Andoverford High uniform back. I won't be needing it now.'

'MICHAEL!' screamed his mum, Millie and Granny May in unison.

'Oh Michael, we're so proud of you!'

'Your grandpa will be looking down on you, smiling my dear,' warbled Granny May.

'Just wait 'til I tell Penny Longfurst about this. This is way better than her new pony!' squealed Millie.

'Thanks,' said Michael, still not really believing what he'd just told them. 'I'm not sure what happens now but we're meeting Bob in the morning our time and we'll find out then. I'll give you a call tomorrow and let you know.'

Michael replaced the receiver. As soon as he and his dad had checked that no one else was around, they both let out a roar that an entire football crowd would be proud of.

'Yeaaaaaaaaah! You did it Michael. You really did it!' screamed his dad, hopping up and down with excitement.

'This calls for a real celebration. Steak house?'

'Perfect. Give me two minutes, Dad. I just need to make another quick phone call.' Michael waited until his dad had left the room, before searching his contacts and dialling the number.

'Hi, Will, it's Michael...er...no I don't really want to talk about what you did. I still think you're a cheat. Just listen. I need to you to do something for me.'

Several racks of bar-b-q ribs later, Michael and his dad sat back in their seats, barely able to move.

'Argh, I've eaten too much,' moaned Michael's dad as he rubbed the distended stomach under his flowery shirt.

'I don't think I'm ever going to eat fries again,' said Michael, with an accompanied burp.

They both laughed and made their way back to the hotel for a sleepless night, full of strange dreams and indigestion.

For their meeting with Bob the next morning they'd been told to go to one of the security offices at the entrance of the FSC, where they would be given 'enhanced access', whatever that meant. The overly serious guard, who was round, bald and unable to stop touching his holstered pistol when he spoke, asked for ID. Michael and his dad produced passports, visas and showed their FSC entry passes, which were scanned, logged and copied. After that, they gave fingerprint and saliva samples, so their DNA could also be stored.

'Best not get yourself into any bother, now they have all your details, Dad!'

'Please move over to IRIS now,' asked the deadpan guard, flicking his thumb to the right.

'Who's IRIS?' asked Michael's dad, looking around the near-empty room.

'Dad, don't be so dense!' hissed Michael, worried that the guard would do something nasty to them if they didn't do exactly as he asked. 'IRIS stands for "Iris Recognition Immigration System"! It's a new technology that uses the unique pattern of the iris in each person's eye. You look into a special camera and the computer scans its database for a match. Once ours are in this system, no one can get in using our names or ID.'

'I knew that,' said his dad, pink in the face as he bent down to look into the small white camera on the desk.

The last security check was the metal detector. Michael laughed as his dad ended up having to have a thorough body search by the humourless guard.

'Yes, as I told you, the pins are out but I still have three metal plates in there,' Michael's dad explained as the security wand beeped furiously.

'Do you have any paperwork to corroborate this?' asked the guard.

'Paperwork? My lower leg was broken in four places. I had two closed fractures of the tibia and one of the fibula. They had plates screwed on them. The fourth was an open fracture, which required the removal of bone splinters, realignment of the bones and the use of external pins to keep the bones in place! These are the puncture marks all over my lower leg. That should be enough shouldn't it?'

Reluctantly, the guard waved Michael's dad through the

metal detector and to a small hatch in the wall. Michael thought that the lady sitting behind the hatch looked like she was out of a Punch and Judy show, with bright red lipstick smothered over plump lips, red circles of make-up on her cheeks and hair piled high on her rather large head. She said nothing whilst she waited for her computer to print something and then placed two plastic cards on the counter.

'That's the way to do it!' said Michael, snorting at his own joke. His dad didn't get it.

Michael and his dad picked up their new passes, put them around their necks and headed for the door marked 'NASA Control Centre – Enhanced Access Only'.

'It feels a bit like we're special agents doesn't it,' whispered Michael, thinking back to some of the spy books he used to read. 'Wonder if we're going to be given watches that detonate bombs or a bulletproof car that can fly? Tom Hill would be in heaven!'

The thick metal door hissed open.

'Ah, there you are! Come in,' said Bob on the other side.

Michael stopped and looked at the room in front of them. There were tens of computers, mammoth screens on the walls, rows of telephones, buttons, levers and more than twenty uniformed people buzzing around.

'Welcome to NASA Control Centre or 'The Core' as we call it. This is where most of the planning and execution of space missions takes place. If you like, it's where we turn our dreams about space into reality,' explained Bob.

Wow! Amazing! Never in a million years could he have imagined that he, at thirteen years old, would be standing in this room, with his dad!

'Now before I explain what's gonna happen next, I just need you guys to sign these confidentiality agreements,' said Bob, handing a sheet of paper each to Michael and his dad. 'I'll give you a couple of minutes to read them through but, basically, you are signing to say that you will never talk about, repeat, write down or record anything you see or hear in this room…and that if you do, you are aware that we still have the death penalty in the United States of America.'

Michael shot a worried glance at his dad.

'It's OK, Michael. He's joking. Florida is a bit more civilised than other parts of the States. It would just be life imprisonment,' he joked.

They both read through the confidentiality agreements and after waiting for his dad to nod in acceptance, Michael signed his name. He hadn't even signed a cheque or anything else for that matter and here he was, signing the official secrets act!

'OK, so here's what's going to happen today,' said Bob, offering them chairs at the back of the room. First I'm gonna take you through a brief outline of the mission to the moon that you'll be training for, Michael. Then at two o'clock we have a press conference arranged to announce your place on the mission. After that, you'll be given remote access to our computer based astronaut training (CBAT), which will mean that you can study and take part in simulations when you're back in England. We've booked your flights for tomorrow and then you'll have two weeks back home before returning to start your training. Any questions?'

Michael was taken aback by the speed at which things were moving and couldn't think of anything to ask.

Bob introduced them to the staff in the room and there was a lot of whooping and backslapping as people congratulated Michael on his achievement.

'Be great to have a Brit up there for a change,' said one man, who carried on entering coordinates on his computer as he spoke.

'Hey, if you like computer games, buddy, just wait until you see the stuff we're gonna have on board the new spaceship!' said another.

Bob ordered some drinks and showed Michael and his dad through to a separate area, with some comfy chairs and a cinema-sized white screen.

'This is our promotional film,' said Bob. 'It's the one we had to show to the government to get the funding and go-ahead for the mission. It's taken us seven years to get to this!'

It started with the first moon landing and took them though all the years of space exploration, right up to the present day. They found out that the building of a new spaceship was well underway and that it would be a mixture of the best features of Apollo and shuttle technology. The idea was that, unlike previous vehicles, this one would be bigger, cheaper, more reliable, safer and re-useable. In fact, the figures Michael saw predicted that the new spaceship would be reused up to ten times. All they'd have to do after a dry parachute land would be to replace the heat shield and then the craft would be ready for re-launch!

'Wow!' said Michael's dad, looking at a sketch of the spaceship. 'It's so much bigger than I imagined.'

'Yeah, that's because it's gonna be able to take four people to and from the moon, deliver crew and supplies to the International Space Station and eventually be able to take six crew on missions to Mars,' explained Bob.

Just like the Mission: SPACE ride they did with Buddy and Carlie, but for real, thought Michael.

'How long will the moon mission be?' asked Michael, suddenly feeling very nervous at so much information being fired at him.

'With the new lunar lander, Michael, it'll be possible to spend up to a week on the moon but for the first one, it'll probably be no more than twenty-four hours or so,' answered Bob.

Twenty-four hours, thought Michael. That's a whole day and night on the small silvery-grey sphere he'd watched from his bedroom window for the last six years!

Once Bob had finished telling Michael and his dad about the Ares I and Ares V rockets, which would get the new spaceship up to the moon, he started explaining more about the objective of their mission. Michael knew all about taking equipment to the International Space Station and about founding the beginnings of a lunar base, but wasn't sure what Bob meant when he started talking about 'identifying the moon's natural resources' and 'key scientific research.'

Once their briefing was over, it was time for the press conference.

'Now, Michael, in about twenty minutes we're gonna make our way down to our "Communications Centre", where the press conference will take place. You'll need to put these on,' he said, handing Michael a pair of NASA overalls and a clip-on microphone. 'I'll be sitting on your right and Rosalind Branton will be on your left. You remember her from the fitness tests don't you?'

Michael nodded, already bemused by the amount of information being heaped on him.

'We've given the press all their questions; so it's just a case of the order they ask them in. I'll run you through the questions and answers in a minute.'

'What do you mean, "given the press their questions?"' asked Michael's dad, looking as confused as Michael.

'Sorry, I sometimes get a bit ahead of myself,' said Bob, pausing for a few seconds and breaking into a smile. 'Any space mission has to be handled very carefully as far as the press are concerned. The government are spending billions of dollars on this and want to achieve their objectives. All the general public are really interested in is who is going up, what their story is and some great pictures.'

'So it's a fake interview then?' asked Michael's dad.

'Not "fake", Mr May, but engineered to get the best out of it for all parties. Here, take a look at the questions and the answers we've put down for you and Michael and let me know if there's anything you're uncomfortable with. We may have time to make one or two changes,' said Bob. 'But the press will get restless if we're late. They've already sat through Jia Li and Buddy's.'

Michael had seen a few press conferences on the news,

usually the parents of a child who was missing or someone appealing for information about a crime, but actually being at one was a bit surreal. To start with, both Michael and his dad had to wear make-up!

'Don't you dare tell anyone about this!' he ordered his dad. He could just imagine what his class would say if they ever found out!

Then there were the spotlights and cameras. Once he and his dad had been seated behind a long narrow desk, the television cameras were adjusted and the spotlights fixed in position. Finally, the journalists arrived and started taking photos of them before they'd even begun.

'Here, Michael. Over here,' asked one of the journalists.

'Michael, Tim, could you look this way please,' said another.

The flashes were just like the strobe lighting on the Space Mountain ride, thought Michael, but he had a feeling this ride would be so much scarier!

They were counted down to the start of the press conference, which was introduced by Bob. He used words like 'amazing' and 'exceptional' to describe Michael. The last thing he felt right now was 'exceptional' but he tried to smile as Bob spoke.

Michael's palms immediately became clammy when Bob opened up the floor to questions.

'Michael, hi, I'm Brad Knowles from CNN. You've had a couple of hours for the news about your success to sink in. How are you feeling about the possibility of being the first ever child to go to the moon?'

'Er…' stuttered Michael, trying to remember the words

he was supposed to use. 'I feel honoured that the American Government allowed children from the UK to apply for a place on the CMP...I mean the Children's Moon Program. I also feel so fortunate to have been selected and am really excited to be working with everyone at the Florida Space Center.' He said this all in one breath.

'Hi, Tim, I'm Jed Carter from NBC. How do you think it's going to be potentially watching your son blast off into orbit in less than two years' time?'

Michael's dad hesitated. He'd been told to do the same as Michael and talk about the pride he felt and the honour of having a place on this mission, but Michael knew that the idea of him leaving earth and flying into the unknown, in little more than a tube made of metal and plastic, terrified his dad. Michael had only been away from home for two nights with the scouts and a couple of nights at Granny May's. This was such a huge thing and suddenly so close to the dreams they'd chatted about.

'Obviously this is the biggest opportunity ever and I'm proud that Michael made it right to the end of the CMP,' he answered, looking over to Michael and smiling. 'But, as a parent, who wouldn't be worried sending their child off into the unknown, particularly when it's that far away!' He was moving away from the script and could see Bob fidgeting in his chair.

The journalists continued to ask their questions, most of which moved away from Michael and focused on details about the mission and its objectives. Bob and Rosalind answered calmly, providing enough detail to keep the journalists scribbling away on their note pads.

A group photograph was asked for, so Michael, his dad, Bob and Rosalind all stood in front of a giant poster of the new spaceship, whilst the cameras bombarded them with flashes. Michael decided there and then, that he would never moan about his mum videoing him ever again!

'Good job, guys,' said Bob after the room had emptied. 'The press got what they wanted and we got some good publicity for the mission! I've put in an order for the national newspapers, so you can take them home with you.

'Thanks, Bob,' said Michael, still spinning from the press conference. 'So we just need to get the remote access for my CBAT and we're finished?'

'Pretty much. We'll sort that out for you now, Michael, then we'll quickly take you through the relocation pack. You can take it with you to read at home properly. Once you're happy with that, we're done!'

Michael hadn't really given any thought to what being one of the final three on the CMP would mean to the rest of his family and his mind started to wander off in all sorts of directions as Bob talked about schools, houses, jobs and the need to live within a twelve mile radius of the FSC. This wasn't just enormous for him; it was going to affect his whole family. Would they want to come to Florida? Could they? What about Granny May? He nodded at everything Bob said but his mind was elsewhere.

Chapter Ten

By lunchtime the following day, Michael and his dad were on their way home. The FSC had paid for them to fly first class. They had their own suite, with two beds, a toilet, sink, televisions, games consoles and as much as they could eat and drink! Michael couldn't wait to tell Adam about it. He would be so jealous!

'Hey, Michael, look at this,' said his dad as they undid their seatbelts after take-off. He pulled three newspapers out of his bag and read the headlines of each. 'American, Chinese and English in Moon Race,' read the first. The next said 'English boy favourite for Moon' and the last headline said, 'May's Moon!'

'Hey look, me on the front page and Chelsea losing to Tottenham four nil on the back. Darren will be gutted!'

'You should keep these to show to your children, Michael,' said his dad, folding them up. 'I wish I'd shared more with you over the years. I'm sorry.'

What should he say to that? He hated these awkward moments.

'I saw that article too, Michael – the one about us as parents. You have every right to be embarrassed and feel resentful. Your mum and I know that we neglected you and Millie.'

All Michael could manage was a watery smile and a nod.

Michael's mum and Millie had arranged to meet them in the arrival's hall. The first-class passengers had priority, so

Michael and his dad were off the plane within five minutes of landing. As they walked through customs towards the exit, bleary-eyed and exhausted from the long flight, Michael's dad started to laugh.

'What's so funny, Dad?'

'Well look at us and then look at them!' he said, pointing to the other first-class passengers around them. 'They look like film stars, producers or mega-rich business people – we look like a pair of tourists, who have been sleeping rough for six months!'

'Yeah, I bet you regret buying those shirts now!' said Michael. 'Particularly when everyone's going to see them in the papers tomorrow!'

'What?'

'Look over there, Dad,' said Michael, part-grinning and part-grimacing.

Just on the other side of the exit sign were rows and rows of cameras, held by rows and rows of journalists. They couldn't even see his mum or Millie.

'No worries,' said Michael's dad, taking a deep breath and pulling in his stomach. 'We're old hands at this, Michael. Come on! Smile and let's tell them how proud and honoured we are!'

'Hey, Mike, do you have a girlfriend? What about Tilly? She gave us a statement saying that she thought you were "hot stuff"?'

'Michael, could you tell us what your friends at school think? Does your training for the next mission to the moon mean that you're leaving the UK for good?'

'Mr May, what exactly happened with your leg and how

has your employer reacted to your resignation?'

The questions from the awaiting press were incessant. What should he say?

Why were they talking such rubbish about Tilly as well?

'Say nothing and keep walking,' said Michael's dad, steering his luggage trolley directly towards a group of six or seven photographers. He didn't stop and as he reached their legs, they parted, like the Red Sea and they were soon through. Michael spotted his mum and Millie, squashed against a pillar, looking fed up and uncomfortable.

'There they are!' said Michael, his heart racing again.

'Michael!' shrieked Millie, running as fast as her nine-year-old legs would take her.

'How do you feel about your brother going to live in the States?' said one photographer, getting between Michael and Millie and forcing her to stop.

'Hey! Get out of the way!' Michael said, stepping around the photographer to hug Millie. He could see her lips quivering and suddenly wanted to protect her.

'We have nothing to say at the moment,' said Michael's dad, suddenly changing his mind. 'Obviously Michael is delighted to have come through the CMP and we are all honoured that he will get to take part in the training for the next mission to the moon. As you'll understand, however, we have just come off a long flight and want to see our family again, so if you could respect our privacy, we'd be really grateful. Thank you.'

Nobody moved and as Michael's dad pulled in his mum, Millie and Michael for a big family hug, they could hear the shutters clicking again.

'Oh, just ignore them!' said Michael's mum, beaming. 'Michael, we were so worried about you doing all of those dangerous and difficult things, but you did it. You really did it and we're so proud of you!' She grabbed Michael again and hugged him.

This is what he'd been missing all these years – the feeling of being a family, a proper family. His mum looked more relaxed and happy than she had in years, he thought. She'd even gone out in public in casual clothes, with hardly any make-up on. That had to be a first!

Once they'd broken free of the chasing photographers and got into the car, they could talk more freely. In the back, Millie started quizzing Michael about the rides in the theme parks whilst Michael's dad told his mum the adult version of events in the front.

'You'd have been amazed, Viv,' said Michael's dad. 'Our little shy boy, who keeps himself to himself, was utterly brilliant! At times he was petrified, nervous, worried, unsure and all that stuff, but he just kept going. Task after task, day after day, he just got on with it!'

They stopped in Presholm to pick up Granny May.

'Go on, Michael, you go and get her. She'll be delighted to see you,' said his mum.

Michael's feet crunched on the gravel road outside Granny May's little cream bungalow. He couldn't remember her living anywhere else, although he knew she'd moved to Presholm when Grandpa May retired, selling the big house in Andoverford. Michael liked coming here, partly because her rules were different and partly because his Granny May was as untidy as he was.

He'd sometimes felt more at home here, than he had at home!

As he sauntered up the path, Michael noticed the jumble of potted plants around a birdbath in the centre of the small square of front garden. They look just like the planets of the solar system orbiting the sun, he thought. In fact, when he looked at the silver wind chimes hanging from the guttering and the spinning multi-coloured plastic windmills sticking up from the patchy grass, he reckoned it looked just like a spare parts garage for space shuttles!

He had to knock three times before she answered.

'Michael my dear!' She was leaning heavily on her walking stick but still managed to pull him over the doorway into a soft hug. 'Come in, my dear. That's it.'

'Actually, Mum and Dad are waiting out in the car. Can I carry something for you?' said Michael.

'Oh yes. There's something I need to you to get for your father first. This way.'

Michael had no idea what she was on about but followed her to the hallway. It was a long, dark corridor, with no windows and a musty smell that reminded Michael of the stench of the wet towels left on his bedroom floor.

'See that hatch up there, Michael,' said Granny May, uncurling her hunched body to point to the ceiling. 'That's the way into our attic. If I give you a pole to pull the hatch down, you can go up and fetch something for me.'

Michael waited whilst his granny hobbled down the length of the hall into one of the bedrooms and hobbled back again with a hook-ended metal pole. He used it to pull down the attic hatch and the ladder inside and used the rail on one side to pull himself up.

'On your right, Michael, you'll see a row of brown boxes,' echoed his granny's voice. 'Go past those and you'll come to some old tea chests.'

'Tea chests…tea chests,' muttered Michael to himself. 'What in the world is a tea chest?'

'Got it!' he shouted, when he came across a waist-high thin wooden box. Crikey! She must drink a lot of tea, thought Michael as he lifted the lid.

'Inside, Michael, are some Hessian bags. You will need to take them out one by one and pass them down to me,' said her faint voice from below.

There were six in total, some of which felt like they could be full of bricks, and others that were very light. Once he'd pushed the ladder back up and secured the hatch, he helped his granny carry the bags out to the car.

'What's in them?' asked Michael.

'Some of your father's old bits and bobs. They must have been up there for at least fifteen years and probably another fifteen in the Andoverford house!'

'Now Michael, I didn't think you'd want to go out after an overnight flight, so I've got some stuff in. You take your granny inside and your dad and I will grab the bags.'

Granny May hadn't stopped asking questions since they'd collected her and Michael noticed that she was wearing the dress she always wore for special occasions. She'd also done a 'Mrs Glendinning' on her hair. It now took on an almost luminous green colour.

Michael unlocked the front door, with his granny still

warbling in his ear.

'Do you really think you will feel safe, going that far away from the earth, Michael?' she asked him, swapping hands with her walking stick to hang up her coat. 'What happens if you break down out there? You can't exactly call out the RAC, can you?'

'No, Granny,' answered Michael, 'not unless RAC stands for Random Astronauts in the Cosmos!' He laughed. 'Cup of tea? You go and sit down and I'll bring it...

'Surprise!' shouted the crowd of voices from behind the kitchen door as he started to push it open.

'Whaaaaaaat!' He jumped back, pushing the door closed again. His stomach felt just like it did on the first plunge of Space Mountain!

'Sorry, love,' said his mum from behind. 'I know that this isn't really your sort of thing but we couldn't ignore how brilliantly you've done.'

A surprise was that last thing he needed right now. A sleep, a shower, a rest for six months – but not a surprise party!

'We've got burgers and hot dogs,' said Chester's familiar voice.

'And sausages and mash!' said a soft Scottish accent.

'I've brought my football!' said Adam.

'And I've got a present for you.'

It was the last voice that convinced Michael that maybe this wasn't the absolute worst idea that his mum had ever had (that was reserved for the disgusting school shoes she'd made him wear in Year Four!).

It was Charlotte, holding a book-shaped gift, wrapped in

Star Wars paper. She was looking almost as embarrassed as he felt.

'Right let's get the party started,' said Mr Rose, sounding really weird to Michael. He was wearing a ridiculous cord trousers-shirt combination that made Michael's dad suddenly seem really fashionable! Having your head teacher in your own kitchen was very strange and an experience Michael didn't want to repeat.

As the other guests appeared from behind the door, Michael saw that about half his class were there, most of his football team and his Uncle Malcolm and Auntie Joyce. He checked to make sure there was no Mrs Jarvis and was definitely no Darren Fletcher!

'Er...I don't really know what to say,' said Michael, putting both hands in his pockets, as he had no use for them. 'Thanks for coming and I hope I don't fall asleep during the party!'

Charlotte stepped forward and gave Michael his present. He unwrapped it slowly, using every second to rack his brains about what to say in thanks. It was a book, *1001 Amazing Facts about Space*. He opened it and on the inside cover was a picture of himself, with the newspaper clipping, which read 'May's Moon,' underneath it. All around the picture were comments from his friends and family. 'Let me know what re-constituted ice cream is like!' Chester had written. 'How d'you play football in zero gravity?' wrote Adam. 'Now I'm interested in NASA!' joked Rosey. Even Darren had written something quite nice – 'Told you your name should be Micky Moon! Well done. Hope you like it up there and don't die.'

'This is great,' said Michael, still looking for Charlotte's entry. 'It's perfect and I'll take it with me to America.' The words sounded funny to him, but he didn't know why. 'Come on then, Chester, let's have one of those burgers you're hogging!' said Michael as the room started to buzz with conversation.

The afternoon flew by for Michael, with no time for him to think about how tired he was. He played football, proved how fast he was by accepting Tom's challenge of a race, and even found himself dancing to the awful tunes that Mr Rose had put together.

Eventually Michael's dad brought proceedings to a close.

'Sorry everyone, but I'm on my knees and when Michael stops that dreadful dancing, I'm sure he'll be ready to collapse in a heap too!'

'Hey! I'm not the one dancing like an over-excited walrus!' protested Michael.

'Anyway, I want to thank everyone for coming and supporting Michael. Obviously he'll say goodbye properly before we leave in September, but from Viv and I, goodbye and good luck in your next year at Andoverford High School!'

It hadn't really sunk in yet that he wouldn't be going back to school. He didn't even know if he was going to have to go to school in Florida or not. It was probably in the pack Bob had given him but it would have to wait until tomorrow now. Michael saw everyone out, thanking Mrs Glendinning for all her support and Charlotte for her extra gift.

How great it felt to climb into his own bed, with his own stuff around him, knowing that he didn't have to rush or perform or be anything other than himself when he woke up. He stared up at the stars on his ceiling and wondered.

It was past midday before Michael surfaced and everyone was already up and dressed.

'Come on, Michael. We're just about to have lunch,' called his mum from the bottom of the stairs. 'What would you like on your sandwich?'

Sandwich, thought Michael – what had happened to breakfast?

'Er...anything,' he shouted back. 'I'm not really hungry!'

After a shower, so long that the water eventually ran cold, Michael almost felt human again and went down to the kitchen for lunch.

'Michael!' said his Granny May as if she hadn't seen him for weeks. 'Now you come and sit down by me, dear, and I want you to tell me the whole story from beginning to end.'

Before long, Michael was in full flow. He told them all about his NBP simulation, his experience on the g-force centrifuge and took special delight at telling everyone how sick his dad had been on the Mission: SPACE ride!

'And how was the swim?' asked his mum, knowing that this was the thing that worried him most.

'Awful! I mean I did it, but if Jamie hadn't helped me, I wouldn't have made it. If I can help it, I'm never going near a swimming pool again!

'Don't listen to him, Viv,' said his dad, 'he was amazing. From not being able to swim a hundred metres without panicking and drinking half of the pool, to doing a thousand metres with breath to spare...I call that brilliant!'

Michael finished telling Millie, his mum and his Granny May the rest of the details of the CMP. There were 'ooohs' when Michael told them about Will's cheating and 'ahhs' when they heard about Jamie's mum, and Millie was in stitches at Michael's impression of Carlie on the Mission: SPACE ride.

'So what happens now?' asked his granny, stopping the laughter dead with her question.

Michael's mum and dad looked at each other with one of those looks that meant 'say nothing' or 'pretend everything's normal', which Michael and Millie both noticed.

'Well, we've got to get things moving, so we're ready to go in two weeks' time,' said his dad quickly. 'Michael, you'd better get on with your computer-based what's it called and read through the pack Bob gave you. Why don't you go and do that now and your mum and I can finish sorting some of the other stuff out.'

Michael took this more as an order than a request and decided that he was probably better off, just getting out of there if his mum and dad were going to have some big heart to heart.

'Come on, Millie,' said Michael, beckoning her to come too. 'I've got something in my suitcase for you.'

'Is she your girlfriend?' asked Millie, as soon as she saw the framed picture of Charlotte standing in the middle of Michael's desk.

'Give that here!' hissed Michael, grabbing it out of Millie's hands. 'It's none of your business!' Why had he left

Charlotte's present lying around when he knew that his sister was so rubbish at keeping secrets?

'I won't say anything if you don't want me to,' offered Millie in a voice that told Michael, she'd need something in return for it. 'I think she's really pretty.'

'Yes, I suppose she is,' he answered without thinking. 'But I don't think she's as keen on me as I am on her. Anyway, it doesn't matter. I won't be around here for long.

'Well she must think a lot of you, if she's gone to the trouble of having a photo printed and buying a frame for it. Perhaps she doesn't want you to forget about her when you go to America.'

'Yeah, I suppose,' Michael said, rummaging in his suitcase. 'Ah, there it is,' he said, pulling out a plastic bag and giving it to Millie. 'Cost me a fortune that did. You'd better like it!'

'Yeah!' shrieked Millie, dancing around in a circle. On her head was the most ridiculous thing Michael had ever seen – a Minnie Mouse set of ears, held on a pink and purple hairband.

'You'll be able to get all sorts of rubbish like that when you come over to America with me!' laughed Michael, putting on the ears and looking in his mirror. 'You can get whatever food you like…and the rides are out of this world.'

The smile suddenly left Millie's face and she thumped down on the end of Michael's bed.

'What's the matter…? Are you worried about moving or what?'

Millie didn't say anything for a few seconds.

'I heard Mum and Dad talking when I came downstairs this morning,' Millie said. 'Well, it was more like arguing than talking actually, so I stayed on the stairs and listened.

'Was it about me?' asked Michael, knowing what the answer would probably be.

Millie nodded. 'Mum's been told that if she leaves her job for more than three weeks, she won't have one to go back to, Granny May is refusing to leave Presholm and Dad's worried about leaving her,' said Millie quietly.

'And what about you?' Michael asked, half-expecting some silly girly answer about not wanting to leave her best friend.

Millie shrugged and played with her ponytail.

When Michael logged on to his 'Computer Based Astronaut Training', he stared at the long list of study modules. He would have to complete fourteen, ranging from 'The Solid Fuel Booster Rocket' to 'Physical Training Programme for Astronauts'. There was even a section on how to eat, drink and use the toilet in space. Chester and Darren would be really impressed, thought Michael. Once he'd completed the study on each module, he'd have to take a test. He needed ninety per cent to pass. That meant studying and passing one every day from now until he went back to Florida in September!

There were also several simulations to take part in, including more work using the Canadarm, refining his skills to operate the payload doors and learning how to deploy the lunar lander.

'There's no end to it!' he muttered, scrolling down the page to the first module.

'Please click on the "start" button and a member of the NASA staff will take you through the module introduction,' he read.

A few seconds after his click, a picture of Bob Sturton appeared in the centre of the page, along with an arrow to start a video. Michael smiled. Bob hadn't said anything about this.

'Hello and welcome to the "NASA Computer Based Astronaut Training",' said Bob's familiar voice. 'My name is Bob Sturton and I'm the senior astronaut training advisor for NASA. Some of you may remember my face. I'm one of the few astronauts who trained for a mission to space, but never got to go!'

'What?' said Michael, frowning at what he'd just heard.

'Yes, having been in training for over two years for my Endeavour shuttle mission, I contracted meningitis three weeks before we were due to go and missed my chance to get into space!'

Michael shook his head. This couldn't be right. Bob had never said a word about this. He listened to Bob's message again. No wonder he'd been so tough on them to make the most of their chances! And now there was a real possibility that Michael was going to do the very thing that Bob missed out on!

The rest of Bob's video gave an introduction to the subject of 'The Solid Fuel Booster Rocket'. Then Michael began to read the training material. He already knew quite a lot about the Ares I rocket, for example, that it used solid fuel for the first stage and then a liquid oxygen/hydrogen mix for the second stage, but the level of detail in this training module was extraordinary. How was he ever going to remember this lot?

After an hour on his laptop, Michael felt heavy weights pulling down his eyelids and logged off. Lying on his bed, he closed his eyes to have a rest but his mind wouldn't let him. He had flashbacks to the CMP. He remembered how devastated Jamie had been and how elated his own dad had been but he'd hadn't really had chance to think about how he felt. It wasn't just about getting to go to the moon, he thought. There was no doubt in his mind that this would be a dream come true, but it was everything else that would have to happen to allow this, that he suddenly thought about. He'd only just started to feel a proper part of his class, with friends of his own. He'd had chance to spent time with his mum and dad for the first time in years. There was the football team and Granny May to think about too.

When Michael woke up an hour later, he went to find his mum and dad. They were at the kitchen table with sheets of paper scattered everywhere.

'What are you up to?' he asked.

'Oh, we're just looking at schools for Millie and working out if you and your dad can go out to Florida first and Millie and I join you for Christmas,' said his mum cheerfully.

'It's going to take some time to sort out renting this house and to be honest, we could do with your mum working until Christmas,' added his dad, not looking up.

'How did you get on with your first computer module?'

'Fine thanks...in fact d'you think you could both come up to my room for a minute?' Michael asked. 'I need to talk to you.'

'Yes sure,' said his dad. 'I could do with a break from all this.'

Michael's mum and dad sat down on his unmade bed and he turned his laptop around so they could see the screen.

'How can you live in this mess?' said his dad as Michael logged onto his CBAT.

Michael looked around his room. There were clothes all over the floor, cups on the windowsill and books in piles everywhere.

'I can't see anything wrong with it!'

Once the CBAT programme had loaded, Michael clicked on the small icon with Bob's picture and then on a tab called 'live chat'.

Within five seconds, Bob's picture filled the screen and Michael started to talk.

'Thanks for waiting, Bob. I've got my parents here now.'

'Oh hi, Mr and Mrs May. How are you both doing?' asked a smiling Bob.

'Good thanks,' answered Michael's dad, shrugging and mouthing the words, 'What are you doing?' to Michael.

'It's OK, Dad, we're on 'live chat'. Bob can see and hear us too,' he said, shaking his head.

'What can I do for you, Michael?' asked Bob. 'Do you have a problem with the CBAT?'

'Er...no, not exactly,' stuttered Michael. He cleared his throat, took a deep breath and tried to speak. 'Er...I've been thinking about my place on the next part of the CMP and...er...the thing is...I've decided that...er... I've decided that I'm going to give up my place… I mean I won't be coming to Florida or taking part in the training at all.'

Michael winced at the same look of complete horror and disbelief on both Bob's and his parents' faces.

'Hey, now hold on a minute, Michael,' Bob said, in a voice that was probably meant to sound calm. 'What you're feeling right now is totally normal. You've just been through a gruelling few months and an even tougher couple of weeks and you probably just need to get some rest. I'm going to give you some time and then you call me back when you're feeling better and I'll talk you through what happens next.'

'No, Bob. You don't understand. I have thought about it and I've made my decision. I don't want this any more.'

Chapter Eleven

'Bob?' said Michael's dad from behind him. 'This is the first we've heard of it too. If you don't mind, we'd like to have a chat with Michael. Is it OK if we speak later?'

'Sure thing. All I ask is that you make sure Michael knows what he's doing and the opportunity he'd be throwing away,' said Bob.

'We will.'

Michael clicked on the stop button and Bob's face disappeared.

'What's going on, Michael?' asked his mum gently.

'I thought this is what you wanted. I thought...'

Michael's mum put her hand up to silence his dad.

'Go on.'

'I don't really know what to say,' said Michael. He looked away. 'Someone like Jamie really needs this chance. I don't. He's missing out because he helped me and because I couldn't prove what Jia Li had been up to. Don't you see...whichever way you look at it, I took a place that should have been his.'

'But you told Bob what you thought and you helped Jamie get through the NBP simulation. Don't forget that,' said his dad. He pointed around Michael's room. 'Just look Michael – everything you love and everything you do revolves around space.'

'I know,' answered Michael. I'm always going to love space and everything to do with its mystery and danger but I need to do this. I need to do the right thing.

Michael wished that there was some way that he could tell his parents the next bit through telepathy because the words were stuck in his mouth.

'Getting on the CMP was one of the best things I've ever done and I'm really proud of myself,' explained Michael, picking up his model of the Saturn V rocket and turning it around in his hands. 'But that was the start of something just as good.'

His parents' faces were blank.

'I got to spend a whole load more time with you two,' said Michael, not looking up. 'I've made new friends at school and football and people notice me now. I'm not just the chubby boy in the corner with his head in the clouds. I'm an expert in something here and people want to be around me.'

There was silence. Michael's mum smiled, but his dad's disappointment showed.

'Michael, you could get all of that in the States and if you're worried about us or Millie – don't. We're all behind you and we just need to work out the logistics, that's all. Think about all the hard work that went into this.'

'Thanks, Dad. I'm really grateful for what you and Mum have done for me,' said Michael and smiled, 'but I've made my decision. I'm going to stay here, I'm going to go back to Andoverford High with my friends and I'm going to play football for my local team. That's it.'

'OK, Michael, but before you call Bob back, can I show you something?' said his dad.

Michael lay back on his bed whilst his dad dashed off downstairs. On the ceiling was a poster of his constellation

– Gemini. He grinned when he thought back to one afternoon at the after school club. He'd been telling Mrs Glendinning all about the school trip to the National Space Centre, when Chester called across the room, 'Any idea what this Gemini consolation is?'

'Yes...and it's a constellation not consolation, you moron!' hissed Michael, fed up that Chester was bothering him when he was trying to work.

'Go on, just give me a few words that I can write down and I'll leave you alone,' said Chester persistently.

Michael thought about it. If he told Chester the answer, he'd be doing Chester's homework for him and if he didn't, Chester would probably keep on pestering him.

'Write this down, Chester, and then leave me alone, OK?' offered Michael.

'All right, touchy,' said Chester, thumping his chair legs back down on to the floor and picking up his pencil.

'Gemini is one of the constellations of the Mars bar. Its name is Latin for bull and its symbol is a sub-machine gun. It can only be seen at a full moon and is shaped like a werewolf.'

As Michael talked, Chester was scribbling everything down in his book word for word. He had no inkling that Michael was talking absolute rubbish and even when Michael started laughing, didn't get the joke.

'Thanks, mate,' said Chester when he'd finished. 'You've just saved me hours of work at home. Mrs Jarvis is going to be dead chuffed that I've finished my homework on time for the first time ever!'

Michael wondered what mark Chester got for his work

on the Gemini constellation!

When Michael's dad returned, he was dragging the six hessian bags from Granny May's attic.

'I was going to give you some of these to take back to Florida, but I might as well give them to you now,' he said. 'I want you to know that I get it and I want you to understand that giving up your place out of some sense of guilt or loyalty is something you'll regret Michael.'

Michael opened each bag and emptied the contents onto his floor. The first three bags were stuffed full of newspaper clippings and photograph albums. He flicked through the first two albums without saying anything and scanned a few of the newspaper articles. The next pile was made up of at least ten round tins with reels of plastic coiled in them. Alongside them was a large wooden box, with a sliding lid.

'I don't understand. Why did Granny May have this lot in her attic? Who does it belong to?' said Michael.

His dad didn't answer, but pointed to what had fallen out of the last bag. It was a small red leather book and as Michael turned it round in his hands and tilted it towards the light, he could just make out what would have been on the front, had most the gold print not worn off.

'It's an autograph book,' read Michael, suddenly getting a whiff of mustiness.

'Open it,' said his dad, with a smile that told Michael he was going to like what he was about to see.

The pages were all stuck together, but Michael carefully managed to prise the first few apart.

'What! Wow! How did...where did...I mean...it says Neil Armstrong here!'

He quickly turned the next page and the page after that.

'Buzz Aldrin…Gene Cernan and Jack Schmidt!'

'You've got autographs from the astronauts who were on the first and last missions to the moon! How did you get these?'

'They're mine. I bought them' said his dad, in a voice that sounded far too casual.

'What?' Michael was sure he must have misheard.

'I was mad keen on everything to do with space from the day I saw the first rocket launch. I just started collecting things from then and didn't really stop until I left home. This lot's been up there for years,' he said. 'Actually I'm glad someone appreciates it. Your grandpa thought it was a load of old rubbish and wanted to get rid of it all!'

'Get rid of it!' said Michael picking up the wooden box. 'Just look at all this! It's beyond amazing!'

Michael slid back the lid and gently lifted out what was inside. He recognised a plastic scale model of the 'Apollo 11 Command Module' as well as its lunar module, 'Eagle'. There was a painted wooden ceiling mobile of the solar system and balsa wood models of both the Enterprise and Columbia space shuttles.

'How did you get all this and why didn't you ever say anything? You know I'd have loved to see this stuff!' said Michael.

'That's why I'm showing you now,' said his dad, holding up the ceiling mobile, so the wooden planets bobbed around like apples at Halloween.

'I just started collecting newspaper clippings and magazines as soon as I knew they were going to land a man on the moon. I did a paper round and odd jobs for my dad, just for extra money and whenever I saw something I could afford, I bought it. Some of the autographs took me years to get.'

'So why was it all in the attic and why didn't you show me before?'

Michael's dad didn't answer. He was still fiddling with the mobile, pushing the planets around on their strings.

'What is it, Dad?'

'Things were different then, Michael. Space travel was brand new and my dreams stayed dreams. There was no way we could ever have imagined the time when a child would get to go to the moon. It was an impossibility back then.'

'So why show me now?' asked Michael.

'Guilt, I suppose. You said you felt guilty about Jamie. Well, I feel guilty that I didn't share all of this with you…that we didn't share it together. Your mum and I were so busy working that we didn't notice that you had something special. I just hope it's not too late.'

Michael didn't reply. There was no reply. He held the Apollo 11 Command Module in his hands like a piece of precious porcelain.

'This is brilliant, Dad. Did you do it yourself?'

'I did the whole lot myself! Actually, I was a bit old to be building this kind of stuff,' he admitted, 'but I loved it! Your grandpa thought it was all a bit of a waste of time so I used to build them under my sheets at night. I remember one particular night I was using a tube of super glue to fix the fuselage to the tail section and got some on my fingers.

I held my hand under the hot tap in the bathroom for ages to try and get rid of it but nothing happened, so I had to sleep all night with two fingers stuck together! The next day, I went to school like that and when I can home, I pretended that it had happened at school!'

Michael chuckled.

'Oh…and what are the reels of plastic stuff in those tins?' asked Michael, suddenly remembering them.

'Oh…now…they're really special,' said his dad, grinning. 'They're cine film.'

'Cine film?'

'Yes, eight millimetre cine-film reels.'

Michael shrugged.

'They used to be the only way of filming,' explained his dad. 'I bought them from a friend's dad for a pound, which was quite a lot of money in those days.'

'What's on them?' asked Michael, dying to know.

'I tell you what. When I've got a minute, I'll get them put on DVD and we'll sit down together and watch them. Deal?

'Deal!'

Michael and his dad talked into the early evening, when it was time to call Bob Sturton.

'Do you want me to stay while you call Bob back?' asked Michael's dad, packing away his space treasure.

'No, if you don't mind, I'd like to do it myself please,' answered Michael, clicking the "live chat" button again.

'Hello, Bob. It's Michael.'

'Hi, Michael. How did you get on?' asked Bob.

'I've talked to my parents and explained everything. I

think they eventually understood and I hope you will too,' said Michael, seeing Bob wince. 'I won't be coming but I want to thank you for everything you did for me. I guess I'll just be another person who didn't quite make it into space!' he said.

The sense of relief Michael felt when he finished his conversation with Bob was immense. It was like a huge responsibility had been taken away from him and he threw himself onto his bed, totally exhausted. He wondered fleetingly if he had made the right decision, but Jamie deserved it. He just hoped that he hadn't disappointed too many people.

He picked up his book *1001 Amazing Facts about Space* and had flicked through half a dozen pages when his 'live chat' call-tone sounded. He flung his legs off the end of the bed and dived towards his laptop to answer before the caller rang off. It'll be Bob wanting to have another attempt at persuading me to give the mission training a go, he thought. Why can't he just accept my decision?

'Hi, it's Michael here,' he answered, preparing himself for the onslaught.

'Hi there, Michael! It's the tall, blond-haired, blue-eyed American who saved you from drowning,' said Jamie, as his picture came up on the screen.

'Jamie! How are you? You look great – like you've been sunning yourself on the beach!'

'Too right, Michael! I needed a rest after the CMP. In fact I was down on the beach when I got a call from Bob. He said you'd dropped out of the programme. How come, buddy?'

Michael gave Jamie a slightly different version of what he'd told Bob and, to make Jamie feel a bit better, put in some bits about his parents not being able to work in Florida and his Granny May needing them to stay here.

'I'm sorry, Jamie. If I'd known all this last week, I wouldn't have put you through the disappointment and stuff.'

'Don't worry about all that. I want to make sure you know what you're giving up, Michael.'

'Now you're sounding just like my dad and Bob!' said Michael.

'No seriously, have you thought about it?'

'Yes'

'And you're cool with it?'

'Yes!'

'Because Bob's just called me and offered me the place, but I wanted to speak to you first.'

'Jamie, go for it,' said Michael, unable to keep a straight face when he saw how excited Jamie was. You deserve it and I think you'll make a fantastic astronaut!'

'Thanks, Michael.'

'Just one thing, Jamie…'

'What?'

'Look after Buddy for me and make sure that Jia Li doesn't boss you two around!'

'Yeah, I will do, Michael. I'll keep in touch and let you know how I'm getting on!'

'You do that and just know that when you're up there,' Michael said, pointing out of his window, 'I'll be looking!'

Michael went downstairs and was happy to just slump

in front of the TV. He needed to empty his head of the thoughts jumping around in it and one of Millie's rubbish girlie programmes was perfect!

'Didn't know you were a big fan of "Ponies and Princesses",' said Millie.

'Mmm...my absolute favourite, Millie!'

Michael heard the phone ring in the hall. It had hardly stopped since he'd got home. They'd had the *Andoverford News* wanting to write an article on his success on the CMP. The *Daily Post* wanted him to dress up in an spacesuit and do a photo shoot down at Cottshill park and even *Sci-Fi* magazine had wanted to interview him about his thoughts on extra-terrestrial beings on the moon! Just imagine the scoop they'd get when they found out that he'd given up his place!

Michael's dad poked his head around the lounge door.

'Michael, it's for you.'

'Who is it, Dad? If it's one of those journalists, tell them to...'

'It's Will. He's wondering if he can talk to you. He says it's urgent and he's waiting to 'live chat' you.'

'What does that cheat want?' said Michael under his breath.

Michael hesitated before pressing the button on his laptop. He was still angry with Will.

'Hi, Mike! How are you doing?' said a cheerful Will.

'OK.'

'Jamie's just called me and told me what you did.'

'Yeah.'

'He's absolutely made up.'

'Yes, well I thought I should do the right thing. Anyway the decision's been made, so don't try and change my mind,' said Michael.

'That's not why I'm calling,' said Will. 'That thing you asked me to do,' he said, 'you're not going to believe what I found out!'

Michael could see that Will was fidgeting in his seat and rubbing his hands together. He thought he might be a bit more subdued after what he'd done!

'I need to show you something. I'm going to play you some video footage first, then I'll explain.'

Michael waited and a small video box appeared. He clicked the corner of the box and pulled it down and outwards to expand. Then he pressed the play arrow in the middle.

To begin with, all Michael could see were blurred white shapes.

'Stick with it, Mike. It's out of focus to start with, but you'll soon see.'

The white shapes gradually came into focus. They were spacesuits. It was an underwater recording of their NBP simulation – not by the NASA divers, but by someone else. He could just make out the faces of Mo, Buddy, Aiko and Jia Li, all looking around for their satellites. The camera moved and suddenly he and Will came into view. They actually looked like real astronauts as they bounced along the floor of the pool.

Suddenly the camera jolted and everything looked like it was behind frosted glass. It panned to the left, then down and eventually settled up and to the right of the person holding it. Michael could make out two people holding on to each other, but they all looked the same. The camera zoomed in.

'No!' said Michael, watching the next piece of footage. 'That's Aiko by the ladder.'

He stared at the screen as the other white spacesuit pulled at Aiko's umbilical and then hooked it over the edge of one of the metal steps of the ladder. As Aiko's air supply was cut off and she started to thrash around wildly, the other spacesuit looked around and then kicked to move away.

'Mike, are you still there?' asked Will.

'I'm still here,' said Michael, unable to say much more.

'Mike, just rewind the video to the point where that person turns around and freeze the frame. Tell me what you see.'

Michael did what Will asked.

'Jia Li!'

There was no mistaking the dark, short hair and permanent grimace of Jia Li. She was the one who had deliberately cut off Aiko's air supply!

'Has Bob seen this?' asked Michael.

'Oh yeah! I did exactly what you asked me to. I told him about Tilly's videoing and about the list of names we heard on Jia Li's MP3 player. He's been through all of it,' said Will, his enormous grin taking up most of his face.

'And?'

'You were right all along, Mike.'

'What?'

'All that Chinese stuff on Jia Li's MP3 player – they were

instructions from her sponsors on who to get rid of! She was to make sure that one by one, all of her main rivals were to fail on the CMP. If she didn't do what they wanted, her funding would be cut and her family dishonoured.'

'What about Matthaeus and Liam?' asked Michael. He wasn't sure if he really wanted to know the answer.

'She rubbed a chest vapour ointment on Matthaeus's goggles, which got into his eyes at the start of the swim. That's the stuff you found in her room. Then she put those laxatives we found in her bathroom in two of Liam's meals! That's why she was at lunch and breakfast with him!'

'Is that just you putting two and two together and coming up with five though, Will?' Michael didn't know if he could trust Will after what he'd done.

'No it's all there on video, Mike. All the proof we need is on film. You know how Tilly was always talking to herself and trying to film us doing stuff. That was all for her reality programme – but she's got footage of Jia Li rubbing the inside of Matthaeus's goggles in the changing rooms. Bob got them tested after the swim. And Tilly's mum was recording the swim. She's got Jia Li slowing down and "accidently" banging into you. They also found two packets of laxatives missing from that box in her bathroom and traces of it still in Liam's system!'

'Wow!' was all that Michael could manage.

'Bob called me whilst you were talking to Jamie. He asked me to get hold of you and let you know. I'm sorry for being such an idiot, Mike. I hope this sort of makes up for things?'

'Thanks for letting me know' said Michael. 'At least we

know we weren't going mad and it was almost worth being locked in a wardrobe for hours with you! Don't worry – we all do stupid stuff. Let's just forget about it.'

'Thanks, Mike. Maybe we can catch up when you're next over?'

Michael said nothing. He couldn't. It had suddenly hit him – if Jia Li had been disqualified then he...

'Michael!' shouted his mum from the bottom of the stairs. 'That programme you wanted to watch is on. Do you want me to record it or are you coming down?'

'Er...coming!' he replied, jumping up from his bed. He was shaking and his stomach felt as if he'd been on the g-force centrifuge again. 'Will, thanks a lot. Sorry. I've got to go. I'll talk to you soon. Bye.' He didn't wait for Will to reply, before switching off his computer and leaping down the stairs, three at a time.

'Oh hi,' said his mum, as Michael sat down with them in the lounge. 'Just in time.'

Michael was silent for a few seconds as an enormous grin crept across his entire face. 'Actually, I'm not really bothered about watching this,' he said...I wondered if we could talk about moving to Florida instead.'

About the Author

Sue Palmer studied German and International Studies at the University of Warwick, before taking up a career in sales and skills training. She has worked with school and pre-school charities for the past ten years and now writes full time at her home in rural South Oxfordshire. Her adventure stories for 9 – 12-year-olds feature ordinary children displaying extraordinary traits as they look for answers and chase their dreams.

OUR STREET BOOKS

Our Street Books for children of all ages, deliver a potent mix of fantastic, rip-roaring adventure and fantasy stories to excite the imagination; spiritual fiction to help the mind and the heart grow; humorous stories to make the funny bone grow; historical tales to evolve interest; and all manner of subjects that stretch imagination, grab attention, inform, inspire and keep the pages turning. Our subjects include Non-fiction and Fiction, Fantasy and Science Fiction, Religious, Spiritual, Historical, Adventure, Social Issues, Humour, Folk Tales and more.